SARA X

Book Three

Double Trouble

Donald A. Shinn

Copyright 2020
Cover design by Donald A. Shinn
All rights reserved.

CHAPTER ONE

Federal Judge Harold Stone sighed as he donned his robes and headed to the courtroom. As he took his seat behind the bench he glanced out at the packed courtroom and frowned at the reporters with their heads down texting away despite his often-repeated court order to turn off all devices. He briefly considered repeating the order one final time, then shook his head and decided against it.

This was his first nationally televised, high-profile trial and he hoped it would be his last. It had been a trial unlike any he'd ever overseen before. Nothing in his experience had prepared him for something like this. Shelby Johnson, a recent presidential candidate had been charged with murder, treason, and multiple other crimes. The world's most expensive and most highly regarded defense team had been assembled, but a prosecution team that seemed more intent on acquitting Shelby than holding her accountable had made their job easy.

Judge Stone had little personal doubt that Shelby Johnson was guilty of all the crimes that she'd been accused of committing. He'd seen the raw evidence in the unpublicized discovery process. He'd watched with dismay as the prosecution had yielded on nearly every motion by the defense to suppress key evidence against Shelby. In the end, he knew that the jury had no choice but to acquit based on the evidence presented.

The trial had been a mockery of the justice system, but such was often the case with a high profile, well-to-do defendant, just not to this extreme. The media was already convinced Shelby would be exonerated and the word he'd gotten from the deputies overseeing the jury gave him no reason to doubt that assumption.

He watched as the jury filed back in with many of the jurors smiling towards Shelby as they walked in and took their seats.

"Members of the jury, have you reached a verdict?" asked the judge knowing full well that they had, or he and they wouldn't be there now. However, the charade of this being a real trial needed to be played out to the very end.

The jury foreperson rose and announced, "We have your honor."

"And what is that verdict?"

"We found Shelby Johnson not guilty on all charges your honor."

The judge thanked the jury for their service and dismissed them and Shelby was freed to resume her life acquitted of all the charges against her.

* * *

Sara looked out her apartment window at the nearby federal courthouse and smiled at the podium set up by the front steps of the courthouse and the crowd gathering there for the post-trial press conference. It would be almost too easy to take out her nemesis from this range with a single shot. Sara hadn't planned it this way, it just sort of happened.

In her line of work, it was important to have multiple safe places one could retreat to if things got a bit hot. This apartment was one such place. It contained multiple changes of clothing, wigs, makeup, and all that was necessary to change her appearance. She also had a cache of weapons here along with multiple identities. She'd had the apartment for over five years and never really cared that it was near the courthouse. Now that might just work in her favor.

She glanced towards her closet and knew that hidden behind a false wall of the closet was her fifty caliber sniper rifle that would make taking out her target very easy. Of course, doing so would lead the authorities to this very apartment and she'd have to abandon it and the materials in it. To kill or not to kill, mused Sara. As the crowd of reporters who'd been covering the trial inside the courthouse rushed out to take positions near the podium, Sara got up and walked to the closet where her rusty rifle was stashed.

* * *

As Shelby left the Courthouse and approached the podium that had been set up for her press availability, her large security detail stood watch, eyeing the crowd nervously.

"I would like to take this opportunity to thank the judge, the jury, and my defense team for their conduct during this sham of a trial," said Shelby. "As I've said for the last six months, I'd done nothing wrong. As the judge and jury saw, the quote evidence unquote against me was fabricated and untrustworthy. I'm only sorry this seemingly reckless prosecution, largely orchestrated by a corrupt small-town sheriff, was able to force me from the race to represent all of America. Being exonerated on election day is at once both satisfying and frustrating. I should now be waiting for the election returns to see if I'd won the presidency, but instead, I shall be celebrating my courtroom victory."

"Ms. Johnson, can you tell us how you feel about Benjamin Schwartz's chances in the election?"

"Benjamin Schwartz is my party's nominee and I support him even though I disagree with many, if not most of his policies. His rants against me in the lead-up to the primaries seem to be at least part of what emboldened the sheriff to target me.

His pick of a far-right, gun-loving, Republican hard-liner as his VP makes me question not only his sanity, but his wisdom. However, as a lifelong Democrat, I refuse to support the Republican candidate even though his policies seem more mainstream and in line with my thinking than those of Benjamin Schwartz."

"Will you be watching the results tonight?"

"Of course, I will, and I'd encourage everyone to get out and vote. Vote for the candidate you feel best represents your interests. And now I must be off."

Shelby waved goodbye and then headed to the five-car caravan that would transport her to the nearby mansion she'd rented for the trial. Her lead attorney climbed into the back seat with her.

"I swear to God if that Socialist lunatic wins this election, I may just kill him myself," muttered Shelby.

"I wouldn't worry about it too much. The polls show Schwartz still behind his competitor."

"And you're stupid enough to believe the polls? We rig the polls to let the public think we're destined to win. The idiotic voters like to back a winner, so if the polls show we'll win, they'll vote for us. The real numbers are a lot closer and some show Schwartz winning. I should have been the nominee. This whole fucking charade was designed just to force me from the race. For what? For an idiot like Benjamin Schwartz to win the nomination? I swear to God I will get my vengeance."

"Just be careful what you say and do publicly. Whoever wins, the presidency will be up for grabs again in four years. You've got to revamp your public image now to be the candidate to take on whoever wins this time around."

"Yeah, I know. More photo-ops of me and babies, kids, and dogs. I know the routine. It's time to be smiling, happy Shelby, even though I feel like ripping people's fucking heads off."

"Where are you watching the results tonight?"

"An old friend of mine, George Strauss has invited me to watch at his place."

"The George Strauss? The multi-billionaire?"

"That's the one. He used to be a member of the Hasselberg Group then he got frustrated and left. I know him from back then. He's been a supporter of mine through his various public interest groups. From what I've gathered he's thrown his support behind the Republican in this race instead of Schwartz, so we'll have to see what happens there."

* * *

Sara watched through her rifle scope as the motorcade pulled away from the courthouse and then set the rifle down without firing a shot. She smiled to herself and muttered, "Maybe another day Shelby. Maybe another day."

While killing Shelby would have felt good, and Sara had kept her in the crosshairs during the whole press conference, there was no real benefit and lots of risk from doing so now. The shot could have been easily traced back to this apartment and would have burned a long time safe house for Sara. She'd have lost everything she had stashed there and the cost of doing so was just too high.

Sara returned the gun to it's hiding place and slid the false wall back into place. She then headed to the kitchen to fix herself some dinner as she waited for the election returns to start coming in. The first polls would be closing pretty soon and she didn't want to miss the action.

The early returns showed the country slightly favoring the Benjamin Schwartz and Charlie Strong ticket and Sara smiled as the results from Pennsylvania were announced.

"The Schwartz/Strong campaign has done amazingly well in Pennsylvania winning fifty-two percent of the vote so far," announced the stunned reporter standing in front of a large digital map of the US with Pennsylvania now colored blue indicating a Democratic win. "We're now able to declare Pennsylvania for the Democratic team of Schwartz and Strong. This is a huge upset as the polling showed Pennsylvania leaning towards the Republican candidate. It's now looking like it's possible for the Schwartz/Strong ticket to eke out a win."

Sara rose from the couch and grabbed her jacket and a burner cell phone. She hopped into her car and drove a few miles away and placed a call to Charlie's cell phone.

"Well, if it isn't Vice President Charlie Strong," said Sara when Charlie answered his cell phone.

"It's not official just yet, Sara," said Charlie, "Don't you go trying to jinx us this late in the game. We've still got a few states hanging."

"You guys have this won. It's all over but the shouting. Who'd have thought two old codgers like you and Benjy could pull off something like this?"

Sara could hear Charlie talking to someone else and then Benjamin shared the phone with Charlie.

"Sara!" said Benjamin. "Damn, it's good to hear your voice again."

"Hi, Mr. President-elect. Are you enjoying this?"

"It's not over yet. I thought we'd lose for sure when Shelby got acquitted this morning and offered that halfhearted endorsement, but somehow it seems to have tipped the scales in our favor."

"Truth be told there was probably nothing better for you guys than her more or less endorsing the other guy. Shelby's not an especially popular person right now. I've been out sniffing the countryside the last few weeks and the states still up in the air seem likely headed your way. You've got this won."

"And a lot of the thanks for that goes to you," said Benjamin. "I was dead in the water a few months back there and you saved my bacon."

"Well, we had a mutual enemy that's now largely been eliminated. Ultimately, I found out what the rest of the voters seem to be realizing, and that's that you're a good man with principles. We need that in this country. I may not agree with all of your views, but you're a good man."

"I may be principled, but I'm still pissed that the jury let Shelby off. So much for my plan to prosecute the lot of them."

"I warned you that juries were unreliable. My way of dealing with people is far more certain. But don't worry, she'll get what's due her in due time."

"You're going hunting again then?"

"No. I'm not planning to. I could have taken her out today at her press conference if I'd wanted to, but I'm over it. It's time for me to step back and try to become a normal person again. It's time to go from being semi-retired to fully-retired. I'm adopting a live and let live approach. If no one's coming after me, I won't go after them. If anyone comes after me, then they'd best be prepared for a fight, but I'm pulling back."

"And you're not worried Shelby will be coming after you?"

"Shelby needs a team around her. Her old allies are mostly dead and gone. She's largely on her own now. I don't see her as being that big of a threat on her own. She's in more of a defensive posture than offensive. If she comes after me, well, that'll be her problem and one I'll fix, but it's time for me to pull back and go back to becoming a normal human being."

"So, I can't call you if a reporter or senator needs a bit of adjusting?"

"I'll take the call, but I probably won't take the job. It's time for me to step aside and get back to the real world."

"You'll be missed."

"You just do the job you're elected to do and fix that mess down there. And congratulations again."

"Save the congratulations for eight years from now when we're done. All we've earned now is one hell of a tough job that may be undoable."

"You two will do fine. I've got faith in you."

* * *

Shelby's security team escorted her to the Strauss mansion which was at the end of a nearly two-mile-long driveway hidden behind two sets of massive iron gates each a half-mile apart with a no man's land between them. Highly armed guards patrolled the grounds and saw to it that no one got close without permission from Mr. Strauss.

The estate was one of the largest on the East Coast and no expense had been spared in creating it. Every interior and exterior surface was of the highest quality possible. The front doors were largely a work of art, each being eight feet tall, nearly four feet wide, and nearly three inches thick of solid mahogany, carved by expert craftsmen into an intricate design.

Shelby was met at the front door by a servant who took her coat and showed her into a luxurious wood-paneled office where a fire was raging. Shelby had once heard that Strauss only burned the finest hardwoods in his fires and she suspected that might be true, though with his kind of money he could just fuel the fireplace with wads of cash.

She was surprised to find Senator Leeds already in George Strauss's office talking with George when she arrived. Senator Leeds had been her top choice for VP if she'd won the nomination and was a longtime friend and colleague. She wondered why he was there though and not partaking in the pending celebration in DC.

"Good evening, Shelby," said George Strauss. "I was just telling the Senator here how disappointed I was when you had to drop out of the race. You two would have won easily had you been able to stay in."

"And now it looks like we'll be stuck with that braindead moron for eight years instead of me," muttered Shelby nodding at the returns on the massive television screen in the office.

George Strauss couldn't help but smile at that. While Benjamin Schwartz was far from his ideal candidate, and indeed he'd opted to support the Republican against Schwartz, George was confident Benjamin's Schwartz reign would be over quickly.

"A Schwartz administration might not be as long-lasting as you think," said George. "I'm quite confident his tenure will expire far more quickly than you think. Then things will go our way."

"Our way?" asked Shelby.

"Yes," said Strauss. "It's time those of us true to the cause united to bring about our globalism ideal. I left the Hasselberg group because they'd become too bureaucratic. I'd know what had to be done, but everything had to go through committees and be put up for a vote. It just wasted time and cost us momentum. That's not leadership. That's not what we need or want. We want a single true leader devoted to our cause. Someone with the vision courage, and wisdom to make the right calls and do so quickly. I know what needs to be done and I'll be doing it. I'd like both of you to join me in this quest. Schwartz will be removed from power and you will take his place.

"The Senator's role as head of the Senate Intelligence Committee and the connections he's made, and you Shelby as the next president of the United States, are valuable allies for me. I'll heed your advice, but the final decision on what to do will be mine. No more committees. No more recording minutes of every meeting. No more computer records to get exposed. Just a small group of like-minded people working together quietly to bring about the world we want. A world where we're in charge. A world where election results like tonight's won't matter. We can build our global empire, and no one can stop us. So, what do you say?"

"I won't be the next president unless something dramatic happens," reminded Shelby.

"Oh, I wouldn't bet on that. I'd be shocked if you weren't president within a few months."

"And how would that happen?" asked Shelby.

"I may just know a few things you don't. Leave that to me for now. Are you both willing to work with me, and me alone, to bring about our vision for what the country and world should be?"

Both confirmed that they were.

"Then we need to get to work," said Strauss. "I've had people monitoring Schwartz and Strong for some time now and I'm pretty sure that if need be, we can get this election result overturned and a special election ordered soon. Things will be looking up for us very, very soon. Senator expect a visit to your office tomorrow from the NSA with some information you'll want to hear for yourself."

"That being?" asked Shelby.

"Our new leaders just got a congratulatory phone call from the most hunted woman in America, hell, the world, and they thanked her for her help and assured her they couldn't have won without her. Their reliance on a serial killing assassin to win the nomination and then the presidency will be used against them. I intend to lure our Sara X into a trap, capture her, and have her turn on those two to expose the truth of what went down, or the version I coerce her to say anyway."

"Were they able to trace the call?" asked Shelby.

"Yes, but it went nowhere. This Sara creature used a burner phone that she dumped after the call. The call was made from an isolated area with no security cameras and lots of access points. It doesn't matter, We'll set a trap for her and catch her."

"She's not an easy person to trap," said Shelby.

"I'm not like everyone else who's tried trapping her. I'm better than they were and I'm a hell of a lot better than her. Senator Leeds and I were just discussing some of the personnel choices Schwartz is about to make. Senator?"

"Senator Dursley was said to be their top choice for Secretary of Agriculture if they won the election," said Senator Leeds. "He has very old ties to Charlie Strong. Dursley has had some marital difficulties of late. His young wife had an affair with a congressional staffer in his office a few months ago. The old boy was having a hard time keeping her happy, so she spread her legs for the aide. The aide got caught and fired and the Dursley's have reconciled, but it hurt Dursley badly."

"And that helps how?" asked Shelby.

"The old fool never got his wife to sign a prenup, so he'd stand to lose half of everything he's got if they divorced. From what I'm hearing he's not trusting his wife much these days and with good reason. She's got a bit of a roving eye. The love he felt towards her is gone and he'd like nothing more than to flush her out of his life if he could find a way to do so without losing half of everything."

"So?"

"Who do people hire when they need someone removed without alimony or other issues?"

"Sara?"

"Exactly."

"And you think he'll hire Sara to kill his wife?"

"Not yet, but I've got a young guy in my office named Dolph who'll bed anyone, anytime."

"The Tripod?" asked Shelby.

"You've heard of him?"

"Yeah, he's half myth, half legend. Everyone in DC has heard of the Tripod."

"He's a handy guy to have around to deal with angry female constituents. He can talk his way into almost any woman's pants and win her over. I'll have a female constituent in my office ready to kill me and the next day she's as docile as a kitten after meeting with Dolph. I'll send him to the Dursley house when I know the old goat is away with some papers or whatnot and see what happens. If things play out as I suspect, he'll bed her, and we'll have what we need. He carries a hidden camera with him to document his conquests and with her on video bedding Dolph, Dursley will have had enough."

"But how does he then hook up with Sara? It's not like she's in the Yellow Pages."

"Word is that Charlie's first wife died mysteriously of natural causes and now I think that natural cause was Sara. That's likely how they first came together with Sara killing his first wife. If I'm right, then Charlie might just recommend her to Dursley and we can catch her in the act of taking out Dursley's wife. With the list of charges facing her, she'd be a fool not to cooperate with us. We could turn her against those two and we could get that special election."

"How do we know Dursley will talk to Charlie about this?" asked Shelby.

"We'll feed the intel to Charlie directly through the intelligence services. Say they caught the wife of the future Secretary of Agriculture sleeping with a Senator's aide while doing a routine background check. Charlie then only has to pass the information on to Dursley. Word of mouth is how Sara found her clients. I'm assuming it still works. There's not much to lose. It's not like Dursley's on our side anyway."

CHAPTER TWO

Heather Dursley heard the doorbell ring and made her way to the front door. Opening it she saw a six-foot-two, young man with a near-perfect physique and a god-like face smiling down at her. Her heart skipped a beat as she saw him and then she regained her composure.

"Mrs. Dursley?" asked the young man smiling at her with teeth so white they nearly blinded her. It took her a second to compose herself before speaking.

"Yes?" asked Heather.

"I'm an aide with Senator Leeds' office and he had some papers he wanted me to drop off for your husband."

"I'm afraid my husband isn't here right now," said Heather.

Dolph smiled as he already knew that. The Dursley home had been under surveillance for several days now and the Senator's travels had been monitored. Dolph had caught Heather's eyes looking up and down his body. Things were going his way.

"Could I leave the papers with you then?" asked Dolph.

"I suppose so."

"They're in the trunk of the car. Let me grab them and I'll be right back. It's a pretty big box."

Dolph walked slowly back to his car and unlocked the trunk to remove the box of documents that Senator Leeds had sent over. The box was unnecessarily large for the papers it contained, but it gave Dolph an excuse to enter the house as the box was too large to hand over to Heather. He shed his suit coat jacket at the car and then flexed a bit before lifting the box from the trunk. The thin shirt he wore did little to hide his muscular build.

He smiled at Mrs. Dursley as he returned to the door and she returned the smile.

"Where would you like me to leave these?" asked Dolph.

"In his office would be best. Follow me."

Dolph eyed Heather's assets appreciatively as he followed her, and he was pleased to see that his prey was younger than expected and seemed to be nicely fit. Many of his conquests were less pleasurable to deal with, but this one could be fun.

Heather opened the door to the Senator's office and stood aside as Dolph carried in the large box. He purposely brushed against her as he passed her then apologized.

"No apology necessary," blurted out Heather, who indeed had felt a bit of an electric jolt go through her from that brief contact. She eyed Dolph appreciatively as he set the box on the floor near the Senator's desk. The possibility that he'd be leaving soon was suddenly an issue for Heather.

"You have a lovely home," said Dolph looking about the office.

"Thank you. Decorating is a bit of a passion of mine."

Dolph already knew that from the briefing he'd received on Heather before coming.

"I don't suppose you'd consider offering me advice on decorating my new condo? I'm afraid I lack a woman's touch in such matters. Oh, but I'm sorry. I shouldn't impose on you in such a manner. It's just that you've done such a lovely job here that it's making my place pale in comparison."

"I'd love to help you out. Are you busy now? I could get us some coffee and we could talk over what you'd like?"

"I've got the rest of the morning free," said Dolph. "And I'd love to have coffee with you. Perhaps you could show me the rest of the house after the coffee so I could get some more ideas from you on what to do at my place?"

"Absolutely!" said Heather. "Let me go get the coffee going and I'll be right back."

When Heather left the room Dolph looked down at the pen camera he was carrying in his shirt pocket and smiled to see that the lens was still pointed in the right direction and the camera was recording. If Dolph played his cards right their house tour would end in her bedroom with Heather Dursley in his arms and the whole affair captured on video.

Heather had taken the time while the coffee brewed to quickly slip into the downstairs bathroom and make sure her hair and makeup were perfect before returning to Dolph with the coffee. Dolph noticed the adjustments and smiled. This was almost too easy.

* * *

Two weeks later.

Charlie Strong was overseeing the transition team and getting routine briefings on intelligence matters when the report on Dursley's wife crossed his desk. Charlie gave the report a read and saw the photos attached to the report and groaned. He felt stabbed in the heart by the report. He knew how much Dursley loved his wife and how proud he was of her. He also knew how much it had hurt him when he'd discovered the earlier affair. A new affair now, would not be good for either Dursley or the incoming administration. They'd kept things relatively scandal-free up to now and didn't need a sex scandal to blow up. Dursley also had been gravely wounded by the earlier affair and Charlie wasn't sure how he'd respond to the news. He knew he had to warn Dursley as nothing in DC ever stayed a secret for long and he didn't want him blindsided by the news. As luck would have it, Dursley was coming in for a meeting later that morning.

Charlie set the report aside and focused on other matters until the time for his meeting with Dursley arrived. Senator Dursley walked in, smiling and very happy.

"How are you, Howard?" asked Charlie.

"Never better," said Howard Dursley. "I feel like a new man with you and Benjamin soon to be in charge. I'm still not a hundred percent sold on Benjamin, but I trust you to help keep him in check. I've got a list of names for assistants for the agriculture job for you guys to look over and run through the screening process."

"Good, Good. We can talk about business in a few minutes. How's Heather?"

"She seems back to her old self again. Things were a bit tense there for a while but in the last couple of weeks, she seems back to normal. She's smiling and happy again. She's looking forward to me getting a new job. It'll mean more time on the road for me, but she's okay with that."

"Yeah, I'm sure she is," said Charlie. He was pretty sure Howard's extended absences in the new job would be only too convenient for Heather and her new beau. He paused for a good long period which got Dursley's attention.

"Is something wrong?"

Charlie hesitated for a few more seconds before nodding his head and continuing.

"It's about Heather. One of the aides of Senator Leeds caught the attention of the intelligence services a while back and he's been tailed since then. I'm afraid he's been with Heather on multiple occasions recently." Charlie slid the file over to Howard.

Howard paused with his hand above the file for a few seconds as he debated opening it or not. He then knew he'd have to know one way or the other. He opened the file and briefly read the report and looked at the photos.

"Shit!" muttered Howard.

"I thought you should know. This guy's not especially discreet and it's likely to become public knowledge at some point. He's got quite the reputation around DC. He's been known to leak affairs to the media himself in the past. I hate having to break this to you, but I didn't see any other choice."

"I swear to God I'm going to kill her for this!" muttered Howard darkly. "She swore nothing like this would ever happen again. She swore on the bible she'd never cheat on me again. Now, she's bedding this guy in my house? Oh, hell no!"

"Just calm down a bit and don't do anything stupid. There are ways to handle things like this. A divorce isn't out of the question."

"And let her take half of everything I own? No. That's not going to happen."

"Maybe she just needs some counseling."

"We've been going for counseling. We were just there last night. She's lied to both the counselor and me. She's been insisting she's being faithful. She's sworn she'd never cheat on me again. I swear to God, I'm going to kill her!"

"No. I don't want to have to find a new Secretary of Agriculture already. We can work through this."

"How? I'm sure as hell not giving her half of everything. I'll be damned if I'll keep living with a cheating whore. What other option is there?"

Charlie paused for a few seconds before continuing.

"Remember my Linda?"

"Yeah. I always liked her, and I know how much it tore you up to lose her."

"It didn't tear me up all that badly. Her death wasn't as natural as you've been told."

"What do you mean?"

"I'd found out she was having an affair with my ranch foreman at the time. I'd head off on a trip and those two would get frisky behind my back. I only found out about it when she started talking to lawyers about divorcing me. One of them gave me the heads up on her thinking about filing for divorce.

"I hired a private investigator and he documented what they were doing on my next trip out of town. Like you, I didn't have a prenup. They were openly planning on what to do with half my estate and laughing at me behind my back.

"I was ready to take matters into my own hands and kill the pair, but the investigator had a better solution. He introduced me to someone who could solve the problem.

"I paid a good price, but the cost was less than a divorce would have been. Hell, it was probably less than the legal fees alone would have been."

"Linda didn't die of natural causes?"

"Not so natural, just made to look natural."

"You paid someone to kill Linda?" asked a shocked Howard.

"Her and the foreman as well."

"Seriously?"

"As mad as I was, they were going to die one way or another. This way it was done painlessly while I was out of state with an ironclad alibi and no one suspected anything. Linda appeared to die in her sleep from a heart attack. The ranch foreman died in a car accident that wasn't truly an accident, but made to look that way.

"If I'd tried to stay with Linda, I'd have strangled her and likely gotten the electric chair. This was my best option. Am I thrilled I did it? No, but I wouldn't have the life I have now if I hadn't done it. She was going to die for what she'd done, they both were, it was just a question of who would take their lives."

"And you think this is an option for me?"

"That's for you to decide. I can get you in touch with the necessary person if you want to go that route, but I can't make that decision for you. I can't even guarantee the person I used is still available, but it's an option. It's a hell of a lot better than killing Heather yourself."

"This information?" asked Howard holding up the file. "Are you sure it's valid?"

"I'm afraid so."

Howard sat there in silence for several minutes then nodded his head.

"Get me in touch with whoever you used. I just pray they can do the job as well for me as they did for you."

* * *

Charlie sent an email to Sara's contact address with the number for a burner phone he'd just purchased to talk with her. He then waited for a reply. He didn't have to wait long.

"What's up?" asked Sara as she called Charlie a few minutes later.

"Is your phone safe?" asked Charlie.

"As safe as can be all things considered."

"I need a favor. A big favor. One you may not want to provide."

"How big?"

"I need you to come back out of retirement for a job. I'm asking as a special favor for me."

There was a long pause and Charlie wasn't sure the connection was still there when Sara finally responded.

"Seriously?"

"I wouldn't ask this for just anyone, but this guy and I have been friends forever. He needs your services. I wouldn't ask if it wasn't important. Things have gotten messy in his life and needs a good cleaning."

Sara sighed quietly while trying to decide what to do. Retirement from the job was nice, but Charlie was an old friend and completely trustworthy.

"I won't say yes or no just yet. I'll look into it. Send me what I need to my email address and I'll see what I can do."

"Thanks, Sara. You're a lifesaver."

"That all depends on one's point of view."

* * *

Sara received the email from Charlie with Dursley's name and address and the pertinent information. She decided to scout the Dursley home and neighborhood beforehand though to make sure it was doable. Her drive into the Georgetown neighborhood had been easy enough with few traffic cams in position to catch her travel. The Dursley house set back off the road and Sara got a good look at it while stopped at a stop sign at the adjacent intersection. No external security cameras seemed pointed towards the access points and there was no locked gate limiting access. A quick examination of cars and vehicles in the area raised no suspicions. She parked nearby and then jogged past the house on a morning run, stopping for a stretch in sight of the house for a longer examination. It all seemed straight forward enough.

Once again, a quick look around revealed nothing alarming, or that would make the job more difficult. She finished her jog, looking for security cameras on adjacent homes or structures that might catch her in the act and saw none that would be unavoidable, then returned to her car. The meeting with Dursley was set for tomorrow, so she'd take one more look around tonight to be sure nothing changed in the hours she'd operate, but for now, she saw no reason not to take the job.

* * *

Senator Dursley had grave misgivings about the meeting with Sara. It was to take place way out in the Virginia countryside at a place even his car's GPS couldn't find. A long, old dirt road was not ideal for his older Mercury Cougar, but he managed to arrive intact at the old, apparently abandoned home. Well, home might be generous. It was little more than an old cabin, likely only containing one or two rooms. The roof was largely gone with gaping holes in it. The front door was ajar. The glass in the windows was mostly broken out.

Had anyone but Charlie sent him here, he'd have turned around and backed out. As it was he seemed to have beat whoever he was meeting here as there was no other vehicle parked nearby. He sat in the car pondering driving away when he saw the front door open and a woman stood there nodding towards him. He got out of the car and walked towards the front steps.

"Mind the steps now, they're a bit shaky," said Sara watching him as he slowly climbed them and joined her. She motioned for him to go inside. A pair of laptop computers were set up in the room catching a feed from cameras that had been placed along the long access road leading to the house.

"I wasn't sure you were here," said Dursley as he took a proffered old wooden chair opposite the laptops.

"I've been here a while and needed to make sure you weren't being followed," said Sara nodding to the laptops. "Charlie told me your story. I just need to know if this is truly what you want."

Dursley had to think about that for a few seconds. His anger at his wife had died down a bit, but he knew he could never truly trust her again. A divorce would take half of all he owned and would get ugly if his wife betrayed intimate details of their relationship. He could become a laughingstock. As a former soldier, he knew death could take anyone at any time and it could come far too easily. He knew he could no longer trust her, he couldn't afford to divorce her, he couldn't live with her, and he'd already decided to move on. This was the best solution.

"It's what I want, if you can truly do as Charlie said you can. I just don't want any of this coming back to me. Spending the rest of my life in prison for arranging the murder of my wife is not a good outcome."

"That won't happen. Her death will appear to be natural. There will be no cause for the police to investigate as long as you do as you're told."

"I'll do whatever you ask. Charlie told me to bring you a spare set of keys, the house alarm code, and the cash."

"You can keep the cash. I'm doing this as a favor to Charlie. I've got enough money these days. I do need to know if there are any guns in the house, any hidden cameras, security cameras, or other things that might cause me trouble. I also need to know about your wife's habits."

"No guns. My wife hates them. There are no hidden cameras and no security cameras. We live in a safe neighborhood. It's very quiet. My wife's habits are simple enough. She drinks a bit of wine most nights to unwind, then applies a face cream before getting into bed. She's usually asleep by ten. She snores like a trucker, but she doesn't think she does. If she's asleep, you'll be able to tell by the snoring."

"Any household staff?"

"We have a cleaning service that comes in on Mondays, Wednesdays, and Fridays, but nothing else."

"You're going out of town soon on a Midwest farm tour?"

"I leave tomorrow, and I'll be gone four days."

"When you get back the problem should be resolved."

"I guess I should thank you. I just never imagined myself doing something like this."

"It's far more common than you might imagine."

"So, I'm gathering."

"You won't hear from me again unless there's a problem. Forget any of this happened and go on with your life. Your problem will be gone when you get back from your trip."

Dursley left the house and drove away. Sara watched on the computer as his car passed the last of her cameras and pulled out onto the main road. She then closed the laptops and secured them in the saddlebags on her dirt bike parked out behind the shack. She pulled on her helmet and the bike jumped to life using the kickstarter. She drove down the path to the cameras and retrieved them and added them to the saddlebags. The bike briefly stalled and when it did she heard it. A faint, distant droning sound, barely noticeable. She frowned and restarted the bike and turned it back up the dirt road towards the cabin. She drove past the cabin and onto what amounted to little more than a dirt footpath leading into the woods.

* * *

"Do you still have her?" asked Senator Leeds of the drone operator who'd followed Dursley's car to the meeting.

"No. We've lost visual coverage of her and the infrared's having a hard time with all the tree branches and growth there."

The later than normal fall had left many trees still with their leaves this late in the season. "I'm just getting flashes of her from time to time."

"Where's she going then?"

"Interstate 95's not far from where she is. My best guess is she's heading that way."

"Damn it! Get our cars heading there, now!"

"Too late," said the operator. "She's there. She just got on and she's heading south."

"Follow her and don't let her get out of sight."

"Yes, sir."

For several minutes Leeds watched as Sara wove her bike into and out of traffic on the busy interstate making it impossible for any car to follow her without drawing a lot of attention to themselves.

"She's clever this one," muttered Leeds to the drone operator.

"Following a fast dirt bike with a car is a lost cause," said the operator. "She knows what she's doing. She just doesn't know we've got a drone following her. She can't shake us in the traffic. We've got her."

They watched as Sara took an exit off the interstate and raced along some city streets and through a narrow alley or two to shake off any pursuers then pulled into a multi-story parking garage.

"Where are the ground cars?" asked Leeds nervously.

"They're about two minutes out," said the drone operator. "They had to stick to the roads and obey the law, so they've fallen behind."

"We've got her then. Make sure she doesn't leave that structure."

He smiled to himself. They had her. Now all they'd have to do is flip her on Charlie and Benjamin and they'd be good to go.

* * *

Sara parked the bike in the garage and shed her helmet. The parking garage served an attached shopping mall. She entered the elevator and got off on the ground floor of the mall and made her way to the far exit. Before exiting she shed the jacket she'd been wearing and undid her ponytail and fluffed out her hair. She then exited out the far door of the mall and crossed the busy street to a nearby shopping center's parking lot where her car was parked. She climbed into the car and drove off.

* * *

"Where is she?" asked Leeds.

"The ground teams found the bike and her helmet, but she's not in sight. They're checking the mall now. She didn't walk out of the garage, so she must be in the mall or hiding in the garage."

"She's in the mall," muttered Leeds. "They'll have security cameras. Get one of our guys in there to check the cameras and find her."

"Yes, sir!"

But it was all for naught as the cameras showed Sara leaving the mall just as the chasers entered the parking garage. There was no footage available of her on any other security camera after she left the mall.

"Damn it!" muttered Leeds at hearing the news. "We fucking had her and let her slip away."

* * *

Senator Leeds was briefing Shelby and Strauss on the outcome of the Dolph affair.

"They took the bait. We were set up to tail her back to her lair and grab her, but she eluded us."

"Did she know she was being followed?" asked Shelby.

"There's no way she knew," said Leeds. "This is apparently how she's escaped detection for so many years. She's clever. We're smarter though. This was just one opportunity to apprehend her, but not our best chance."

"She just left the bike there?" asked Shelby.

"She'd bought it online for a few hundred dollars. The seller didn't know who she was. She showed up with a helmet and the cash, so he sold her the bike. He got a good price for it and that's all he cared about. We've got people watching the bike in case she comes back to reclaim it, but she's likely not concerned about losing it."

"What happens now?" asked Shelby.

"We believe the hit is to go down while Dursley is on his Midwest farm tour," said Leeds. "We'll have people in place waiting for her to show up and ensure that we catch her in the act. Then it's just a matter of getting her to talk."

"Which should be no problem," assured Strauss. "They always talk. They don't think they will, but we'll wear her down until she does. No one resists forever. Holding her will give us leverage over the administration that could be quite useful. If nothing else, we can expose the truth and force a special election. It was foolish of them to expose their campaign to someone like her. We'll take advantage of that mistake."

"When you capture her, I want to be here for the questioning," said Shelby.

"It won't be a gentle questioning I'm afraid," said Strauss.

"I'll rip her fucking skin off myself if that's what it takes. I want to watch her suffer after all she put me through."

"So be it."

* * *

Dursley left on his Midwest tour and Sara drove through the neighborhood the morning he left to see if anything had changed. She wasn't happy with what she saw. New vehicles were along the street and many more than normal. A few of the vehicles had people inside them which was highly unusual for this neighborhood. She drove away and pondered the situation.

Was this a trap, or had she caught the neighborhood at a bad time? She'd come back that night to be sure. On her return trip, many of the same vehicles were in the same spots with people still inside. This was an ambush just waiting for her to act on killing Dursley's wife. This was a trap of some sort arranged by someone, but who? Charlie? No, not Charlie. Howard Dursley had rung true to her also.

Only those two should know of the planned operation, but clearly, someone else did too. If neither Charlie nor Dursley had told anyone, then those now waiting in ambush must have overheard the planning somehow. The meeting with Dursley had been safe enough but the feeling that she'd been watched and that low-level droning sound she'd heard had alarmed her. Still, they'd have to have known of the meeting before it happened to have a drone in the air.

She'd been using a burner phone on the call with Charlie that should have been untraceable and the email address she'd given Charlie to use was unique and should have been safe. She thought everything through and concluded a listening device in Charlie's office must have been the source of the leak. There was no other hole in the system.

She drove away from the Dursley house and used a burner phone to call Charlie on his burner phone.

"Hey, Charlie. I can't do what we talked about. It looks like someone's been overhearing our conversations. You might want to look into that."

"It's a no go then?"

"No. It's off. It was a trap. We were set up."

"It was a trap? Dursley?"

"I don't get that vibe from him," said Sara. "I'm thinking it's someone else."

"Thanks for trying. I'll let him know when he gets back."

"Be careful what you say for a while. I'll be looking into things a bit to try and find out who's eavesdropping on you. We might just be able to unravel this pretty quickly."

"Be careful."

"I always am."

She hung up the phone, threw it into a storm drain, and drove off. She had some research to do and had a good idea of where to start looking for answers.

* * *

"Son of a bitch!" muttered Senator Leeds as he heard the tape of Charlie's side of the conversation. "How did she know it was a trap?"

"Your people were probably too obvious," said Strauss. "She's not a fool this one. She's not as smart as we are, but she's not a fool."

"So, what do we do now?" asked Shelby.

"We pull back the watchers and hope for the best," said Strauss. "We'll find her, contain her, and get the answers we need eventually. Given what we already know about her and the Schwartz/Strong campaign, we might have enough to force them into playing by our rules even without physically detaining her or flipping her. That phone conversation we have on tape is pretty damned convincing."

"But, no names were mentioned and for all anyone outside of us knows, he could have been asking her to do anything."

"Who calls a professional killer to do anything but kill? If we leak that tape, or threaten to leak that tape, to our media allies, it will give us power over those two morons."

* * *

Dolph awoke from his nap to a gentle knocking on his door. He opened the door to find an attractive woman standing there. He'd had no real plans for the night, but that might be all about to change.

"Can I help you?" asked Dolph as he subtly flexed his muscles hoping to impress this potential conquest.

"I sure hope so," said Sara as she removed the stun gun from her purse and zapped Dolph. He fell backward into the room. Sara entered the room and closed the door behind her. Sara quickly secured Dolph's arms and legs with Kevlar reinforced zip ties. She gagged his mouth to limit his ability to shout and then started to search his condo. She found the gun safe in his bedroom and smiled at the electronic lock securing it. She placed her electromagnet over where the electrode was to unlock the safe and turned it on. The magnet did its job and the safe door swung open.

She removed the forty-five-caliber handgun with Dolph's name engraved on the barrel that he'd proudly displayed on his social media posts. She checked to be sure it was loaded and slid it into the waistband of her pants before returning to find Dolph struggling against his bonds.

"Don't even think about breaking those zip-ties. They're reinforced with Kevlar threads, so they just don't break. I could hang this whole condo from one and the damned thing wouldn't break. They cost a ton, but they're worth every penny.

"Now, I'm going to ask you some simple yes or no questions and you'll answer by nodding your head yes or shaking it no. Easy, huh? And if you don't answer the questions then I'll start cutting off bits and pieces fo you until you do. Are you ready to begin?"

Dolph glared at her for a second and then nodded his head.

"You are having an affair with Heather Dursley. Is that correct?"

No reply came immediately then Sara pulled out a long knife and pressed it against his crotch eliciting a response. A nod was the response.

"Was this affair your idea?"

A shake was the answer.

"No, I thought not. She didn't seem your type, not that you seem all that discriminating. So, was it your boss's idea?"

He refused to respond.

Sara pressed the knife harder against his crotch.

"You really should think about answering my questions. Things could get a mite bit unpleasant for you if you don't."

Dolph looked at the placement of the knife and then nodded.

"It was Senator Leeds' idea then?"

A quick nod was the response when Sara pressed harder on the knife.

"Now we move onto the why. I'm assuming this was a trap to ensnare me?"

A nod was the response.

"Is Senator Leeds the one listening in on Charlie's private conversations?"

A shake of the head was the answer.

"Does he have someone listening in for him?"

A nod was the reply.

"Is the trap still set?"

A shrug of the shoulders provided the answer.

"You don't know?"

He nodded his head.

"In that case then, I think we might just have to go and find out. Maybe you can see old Heather one final time too. What do you think of that?"

Dolph merely shrugged.

* * *

Senator Leeds was in his office when his secretary advised him that Dolph hadn't shown up for work and she couldn't reach him on his cell phone.

The Senator had an FBI source track Dolph's cellular phone and the FBI reported it was at Senator Dursley's house. Leeds felt his heart sink at that moment as an inkling of what lay ahead crossed his mind.

"Get my car," he said to his secretary as he was pulling on his coat and preparing to leave the office. He was soon headed to the Dursley house, but it was too late. The local police had already arrived and established a perimeter.

"What happened here?" asked the Senator.

A detective came out and explained that there had been an apparent murder-suicide. The cleaning service had shown up that morning and found the pair dead. It was pretty cut and dried. The note from Dolph made it clear that he couldn't live without Heather Dursley and her decision to stay with her husband over Dolph was too much for him. He'd shot Heather Dursley twice in the head and then turned the gun on himself. His handgun had been used for all the fatal shots and there was no indication of foul play. The only fingerprints found at the scene were those of Dolph and Heather Dursley. Gunshot residue tests indicated that Dolph had held the gun and fired the shots. It was pretty much an open and shut case.

"Son of a bitch," muttered Senator Leeds as his driver drove him away from the scene. "Take me to the Strauss Mansion."

George Strauss was waiting with a glass of scotch when Senator Leeds arrived.

"I'd figured you'd need this," said Strauss.

"That fucking bitch did this!"

"She's good, I'll give her credit for that. She finished the job after we pulled the trap away. She's a clever girl. Care to bet she questioned Dolph before she killed him?"

"He knew next to nothing."

"Next to nothing isn't nothing. You could be at some risk now. You'd best be careful."

"I've got good security in place. This isn't over. The police will figure out it's not a murder-suicide."

"I doubt it. They always look for the easy answer. A murder-suicide is the easy answer in this case. Dolph's gun was used. He was there. He went in wanting to resume the affair and she refused. He threatened her. She stood her ground. He shot her, then became so upset he shot himself after writing the confession. That's the easy answer. That's what they'll believe. Why wouldn't they believe it? There are no one else's fingerprints around. Dolph's house wasn't ransacked. The gun safe had been unlocked. Hell, even knowing it was set up, I'd be hardpressed to believe it wasn't a murder-suicide."

"So, now what?"

"We wait, we watch, and we learn. We haven't lost the war, just the first of what promises to be many battles. She claimed the first victims, but we've got lots more soldiers. We'll win this fight. We'll get that special election and when we do, you and Shelby will reclaim your rightful place."

* * *

Craig Burke, current CEO of Bentley Security, awoke feeling remarkably refreshed. So refreshed in fact that he couldn't remember the last time he'd felt that good. Then he remembered the last time he'd felt that way and groaned. He tried to move his arms and his fears were confirmed.

"Sara, if you're nearby and want to talk about something I'm awake now," said Craig.

"Ah, good," said Sara entering the bedroom with a teacup in her hand. "I was just fixing myself a cup of tea. I know you and your guards are more coffee drinkers, so I didn't fix any for you all. By the way, I know we've talked about this before, but that's a bad habit you'll have to break. You've all been lucky it's just me who's caught onto that and has drugged your coffee before you arrive at that store. If I was a bad guy, you could all be in trouble."

Sara had previously drugged Craig and his men by drugging the coffee they picked up at a nearby convenience store on their way back to his house, so the experience wasn't a new one for him.

"Thankfully, there aren't that many people out there looking to drug me and my guards. You know, you don't have to do this to get to talk to me. There are things called phones, emails, texts, and the like."

"What can I say, I like the personal touch. I'm not a big fan of using devices where others could be listening. I'm finding that lots of the wrong people seem to be getting information these days from electronics."

"I will say that whatever it is you use to wake me up does the job. I should pay you to drop by every morning and hit me up with some."

"The long-term side effects would be a bit messy if you used it consistently. You don't want to get addicted to that stuff and it can prove addicting. I do however have a question about communication security that I hope you can help me with. I know you guys at Bentley Security are good with the electronic eavesdropping. I also happen to know that Charlie's office and likely his other means of communication are being monitored. I'd be interested in knowing if Bentley is behind it."

"He's being monitored? How do you know?"

"I know. That's all you need to know. What I don't know is who's behind it?"

"We're not doing it. If anyone's doing it it's likely one of the Five Eyes partners."

"Five guys?"

"No," corrected Craig, "Five Eyes. The five eyes are Canada, Great Britain, New Zealand, Australia, and the United States. It's an intelligence-sharing alliance that was set up back in the fifties but still lives today. Sensitive, in-country spying is done by one of the allies who then report back the findings to the originating country. When Princess Diana was dating Dodi al-Fayed, we spied on her and reported their conversations back to the Brits. The Brits have spied on our people in return when asked. Australia, New Zealand, and Canada kick in when they can help also. It's mostly a US and British setup though."

"How does it work?"

"Everything electronic is collected these days and I mean everything. The NSA has a facility in Fort Meade that sorts through it all and finds whatever nuggets anyone's looking for. They can sort by who sent it, who received it, keywords or phrases, and even voiceprints. It's impressive what they can do. Their biggest issue is sorting it all out to find the good stuff. Any chance you could untie me now?"

Sara nodded and came over and flicked open her knife and cut the restraints binding Craig's arms. He sat up and flexed then continued.

"If anyone's monitoring Charlie's communications it's likely the British. There's a desk in Fort Meade where all five partners have chairs and all any of the partners have to do is make it known who they want information about and one of the partners will pick up the ball and deliver whatever they can find."

"Why not just do it yourself?"

"All five countries have rules against spying on their citizens. So, they don't. They simply have a partner do the spying for them and prepare them a report."

"That's kind of sneaky."

"But effective. It's been done that way for over a half-century. You think they're spying on Charlie?"

"Someone is. I was hoping it wasn't you guys and I'll take your word for that for now."

"I might be able to find out more for you if you're interested. I've got a few former NSA guys on the payroll who know a lot more about this stuff than I do. They still have connections inside the Five Eyes alliance. They can probably get me more details."

"That would be good. I need to know who's behind all of this."

"I'll see what I can find out, but it'll come with a price."

"What kind of a price?"

"No more knockout visits. It's kind of tough on my ego to wake up tied down to one's bed."

"Some men like that sort of thing, but it's all right. I guess I can agree to that. That's it?"

"That's enough for me."

"How do I get the report from you?"

"There are a pair of scrambled satellite phones in the top left desk drawer. Grab one of those and when I've got the report, I'll give you a call and we can set up a dead drop."

"They can't tap those phones?"

"I won't say they can't, but it takes them longer. By the time they do, we should have made the exchange, and both be gone. Just dump the phone when the call's done and you should be safe."

"Any ideas on how to communicate with Charlie without it being monitored?"

"The safest option is to meet in the safe room at Bentley Security. It was built to withstand even the most intensive snooping. No one can eavesdrop on anything that happens there."

"Yeah, I don't see myself waltzing into Bentley Security headquarters what with half of the staff still looking to kill me. I might recommend Charlie and Benjamin meeting there to discuss strategy. I still need a safe way to communicate with them without getting myself killed in the process."

"Nothing's a hundred percent safe. Courier delivered notes might be your best option, but the courier could be intercepted if you used the same one consistently and getting past security now that's he's the VP-elect might be challenging for a courier."

"I might know a way to make that work."

"Is that food I smell?"

"I cooked you up some bacon and eggs. They're in the kitchen on a plate. I've got to get running before your guards wake up. Give me a buzz when you've got the info I need."

"It shouldn't take long."

Sara grabbed the satellite phone from the drawer and left Craig's home as he got to his feet and stretched. He headed to the kitchen and examined the food then decided to eat it. It's not like Sara to poison him twice on the same day and the food smelled too good to throw away. Once done he'd have to go and rouse his security detail then head to the office to try and get the necessary information.

* * *

FBI Special Agent Amy Jeter felt very special indeed. Her relationship with fellow FBI agent Paul Warburton had been kept hidden from their fellow agents and superiors. Paul was a slow, kind, and patient lover who never failed to fulfill her. She stroked his back as he lay sleeping alongside her in the bed. She would be wound up like a kite after their love-making and unable to sleep for hours, but he would drift off into the deepest sleep imaginable. She'd discovered she could even run the sweeper in the room without waking him up.

She felt incredibly lucky to have hooked up with him and the two were now talking about long term plans. Paul and his wife, while still technically married, had been separated and talking of divorce for quite a while and the marriage only still existed in name.

Both agents had come through the training at Quantico together and formed a friendship there. That friendship had grown and evolved into a rivalry and now what now looked like a real relationship. Amy and Paul had both advanced up the ranks of the FBI and jokingly challenged one another to top the other. Paul had gotten the most recent promotion and was now just ahead of Amy in the race to the top, but rumor had Amy leapfrogging him soon with the new administration coming in. She had a few connections in the Benjamin Schwartz camp that she was hoping to exploit.

Amy rolled onto her back and let out a long sigh. Both she and Paul had climbed high enough in the hierarchy that they were seldom in the field and facing any danger. To some extent, Amy missed the thrill of that, but the fear when Paul was in the field was worse than the thrill she felt herself. Both now being largely out of the line of fire was by far the best outcome, but Amy still missed that thrill.

* * *

The report back from Craig Burke didn't take long to arrive and it told Sara all that she needed to know. The transition team was being spied on by our allies in the Five Eyes alliance and everything Charlie, Benjamin, or any of the other top people in the transition team said/did was being reported back to Senator Leeds of the Senate Intelligence Committee through his sources in the intelligence community. From Leeds, everything went to both Shelby Johnson and George Strauss.

Sara was waiting near the airport when Julio, Charlie's ranch foreman, flew in for his weekly briefing to Charlie on how things were going at the ranch. Sara intercepted him as he was on the way to the hotel where Charlie was running the transition team.

"Remember me?" asked Sara as she appeared before Julio.

"Yes, Ma'am. Am I in trouble?"

"No. I need you to do me a favor. Give this note to Charlie when you see him and no one else. I mean no one else. Understand?"

"Yes, Ma'am."

Sara melted away into the crowd and watched from a distance as Julio placed the note in his pocket and headed into the hotel.

"Julio!" said Charlie warmly. "Welcome to DC. Did you get that fencing on the back forty fixed?"

"All fixed and good as new."

"Damn, I miss that ranch already. What's that?"

Julio handed him the paper Sara had given him. Charlie read it and muttered a few choice curses.

"Everything okay, boss?" asked Julio.

"Yeah, everything's fine. I just found out something I didn't want to hear. Thanks for this by the way."

"I've learned not to say no to that lady."

"You're a smart man. Let me grab a pen and some paper and I'll write down what I need you to do back at the ranch. It won't take more than a few minutes then I'll let you go out and see the sights."

Charlie wrote the reply to Sara and handed it to Julio along with a note explaining that his offices and phones were being monitored, so they couldn't talk freely. Julio was to meet with Sara at the Smithsonian Air and Space Museum to deliver the response.

* * *

Sara's note said, "Confirmed, Five Eyes watching/listening to you. It seems to be the British desk. You must be careful what you say and do in/around your office, home, or elsewhere. Everything is going directly to Leeds/Johnson/Strauss. All communication should be done by courier. Suggest importing Marley and your guys as dog walkers. We can rendezvous in parks to exchange messages that way without drawing undue suspicion. Strongly suggest you/Benjamin contact Craig Burke of Bentley Security for more info. He's got a private meeting area you can use to talk freely among yourselves. Send a reply by Julio as courier to the Air and Space Museum. If he's not followed I'll meet him there. Be careful!"

* * *

Sarah watched from the windows of the Air and Space Museum as Julio arrived. No one seemed to be following him. She rendezvoused by the Apollo Mission display and Julio handed her Charlie's reply which she quickly read, thanked Julio, and then headed out of the museum. She used every trick she knew to ensure she wasn't being followed and then made her way back to one of her safe houses to wait for the game to play out.

The news reports of the murder-suicide of Senator Dursley's wife and Dolph was getting a lot of news, but Dursley was playing his role brilliantly. He'd been pulled back from his Midwest farm tour when the bodies had been found and was now playing the grieving husband role perfectly.

* * *

Charlie made a call to Bentley Security and got through to Craig Burke who agreed to meet with both he and Benjamin. The phone call made it sound like the new administration was looking to outsource the security guards at federal prisons and Bentley was under consideration and the two would like to meet to discuss the topic. Both sides knew the real cause of the meeting was anything but business. Craig Burke knew that having powerful friends in leadership could be helpful to his company and there were few in DC more powerful than the newly elected president and VP.

The motorcade arrived at the Bentley Security headquarters and their security team ushered them into the building. Both men were screened by Craig's electronic security detail to ensure they didn't have any listening or tracking devices currently on them before they were led upstairs. The security detail was forced to remain in Craig Burke's office while the other three went upstairs.

"I take it Sara got in touch with you then?" asked Craig when they were finally in a safe place to talk.

"She said Five Eyes was watching us and to get in touch with you," said Charlie.

"She's right. The Brits have taken the lead. The other three are being largely kept in the dark. Everyone on your staff is being monitored. I've got transcripts of what's been sent over there on the desk if you're interested in knowing how intense the surveillance has been."

"Why are they doing this?"

"My best guess, based on what I've heard, would be that they're planning a coup to overthrow your administration and then call for a special election where they'll stack the deck for Shelby to win."

"How do you know this?" asked Benjamin as he began leafing through the data.

"A lot of it is in those files. One of my intel guys worked at the NSA and had a thing with one of the women on the New Zealand desk at Five Eyes. They're still close and she's cooperating with us on this. The others on the desk don't give her a lot of respect and she's taken it personally, so anything she can do to sabotage them is fine with her."

"And she's not playing us?" asked Benjamin.

"If she is, then she's damned good at it," said Craig Burke. "She's now monitoring the communication between Shelby, Leeds, and Strauss and sending us what she gets in addition to what they get on you guys. No one assumes she's competent, so she's trying to prove them wrong."

"So, we know they're listening to us," said Benjamin, "and now we're listening to them, but they don't know we're listening to them. That could be helpful. We could use that to our advantage."

"We also have Sara on our side," reminded Charlie. "We could have her just eliminate the problems."

"It's not that easy," said Craig Burke. "Shelby and Strauss have vastly increased their security. Getting to either of them, even for Sara, would be difficult at best."

"Besides," added Benjamin, "I'd like to take these bastards down legally and put them away for once and for all. Sara could kill them, but I want them to face the music for what they're plotting."

"They want Shelby back in power with Leeds as her VP," said Craig. "I'm not sure that's good for any of us."

"Leeds might be an interesting angle," said Benjamin. "He's a power-mad politician. Suppose we offered him a role in our administration that would put him in the line of ascension? Say, Secretary of State? He can't very well call for a special election if he's part of the administration and given he could assume the role of President should both of us and the House Leader get taken down, he'd likely be happy about that role. The House Leader's one of his pets anyway, so he could just slip into the VP role if the House Leader became President."

"Do you want that sleaze-ball in our administration?"

"He might as well be, he's getting all of our information anyway. We could keep a closer eye on him with him on the inside."

"What about the prosecution though?" asked Charlie.

"There's an up and comer in the FBI who some of my people are very high on. Her name is Amy Jeter. They say she could be the first female director given her trajectory. As far as I can tell she's clean and honest. If we could get her this information, she might just have the balls to take on Leeds, Shelby, and Strauss. No one in the current DOJ will go after them, that's for sure."

"How do we get the information to her?"

"Sara?"

"Would she do it?"

"I would think so."

"Okay then, let's pack it up, find a place to stash it and then get word to Sara through your new messaging system and see what she says."

"Leave it to me to stash it," said Craig. "You guys are being followed too closely. Just let me know where you want the stuff stashed and I'll see to it that it's there when you need it there."

"No traps or games though," said Charlie.

"I'm not that stupid. Sara's smarter than the rest of us. She'll find a safe place to make the stash and tell you where, and when to have it there. I'll deliver it myself, so there's no one else involved. I'm assuming we're only sending this FBI agent the coup related stuff and not your internal communications?"

"That's right."

"It's not that big of a package then. I'll sort it all out and have everything ready when I hear back from you guys."

* * *

"What are Tweedle-dumb and dumber doing at Bentley?" asked Leeds of his team monitoring the pair.

"It looks like Craig Burke is giving them a tour of the place. They went into an elevator in his office and disappeared somewhere. We lost them on the drone, but the watchers outside said they haven't emerged. They're in there somewhere. Wait a minute, the elevator door is opening again. There they are."

"Any changes?"

"No. They look the same as always. Burke's shaking their hands and showing them to the door. Whatever the meeting was about it's over. It looks like they're leaving."

"Keep following them. I need to know everything they're doing."

Craig Burke watched out of his office windows as the three-car motorcade carrying Charlie and Benjamin sped away. He wasn't surprised to find four additional cars pull out and follow the motorcade.

"Those two are in one heap of a lot of trouble," mused Craig. He thought over the odds of them staying in power against the Leeds/Strauss/Shelby triumvirate and frowned. The odds weren't in their favor. Of course, they did have a few hole cards to play that could change the game. He headed back into the elevator to put together the package for Sara. She should be getting word later today or tomorrow and then decide on the location for the pickup. Would she make the pickup? He pondered that for a few seconds and then smiled. Yeah, she would. She'd want to help Charlie and Benjamin.

* * *

Sara scouted the park near the transition hotel and soon spotted her target. An older German Shepherd was being walked through the park. She skirted the perimeter of the park and looked for observers and noted what she saw, then headed into the park where the dog walker was now seated at a bench. As she approached the pair, the dog turned his attention towards her and gave his tail a wag as a familiar scent met his nose. Sara reached down and rubbed the dog's head behind his ears and asked, "How's it going, old-timer?"

Marley responded by climbing onto his hind legs and placing his front paws on Sara's shoulders as he licked her face.

"Enough of that," said Sara after a few seconds and eased the big dog down. She nodded to the dog walker and said, "Long time no see."

"About six months now. You're looking good. I understand there's some trouble brewing?"

"Just a coup attempt, nothing too big," replied Sara jokingly. "I see you brought friends."

"Six watchers around the park, six more standing by in vehicles outside the perimeter with more firepower if needed. It pays to be prepared. If anyone tries anything we should be able to deter them."

Indeed, this same team had forced the jet carrying Shelby Johnson to make an emergency landing and had defeated Bentley Security's private army on an earlier occasion including taking out helicopters and armored personnel carriers. They'd proven their value. It was almost a shame to reduce them to dog walkers, but Marley presented the perfect way to pass information to Charlie.

"Do you know the plan?"

"We walk Marley, you make contact, slip whatever you need Charlie to know into Marley's collar and we return Marley and the information safely to Charlie."

"Sounds about right. It's not the most exciting assignment I'm afraid."

The leader smiled before replying. "I have a feeling it'll get more exciting since you're involved. Things don't stay quiet around you for long."

Sara smiled at that and then slid the paper with her notes under Marley's collar as she hugged the big fellow one more time.

"Take care," said Sara as she rose and walked away from the bench.

"Okay, big guy," said the leader to Marley. "Our job here is done. Let's head back to the hotel."

* * *

The arrival of Marley had not gone unnoticed by those working for Senator Leeds.

"He used his private jet to fly in his dog and a dog walker?" muttered Leeds. "Some people just have too much money."

"What do we do about the dog?" asked his aide.

"Nothing. What's the dog going to do? I'm surprised he hasn't flown in his wife instead of the dog. I guess that shows you where his priorities are."

"You know what they say about DC. You can only trust your dog."

* * *

FBI Special Agent Amy Jeter awoke feeling especially refreshed and went to stretch only to find that her arms wouldn't move. She opened her eyes and saw that they'd been zip-tied together and then zip-tied to the headboard. A moment of panic surged through her then she looked over to Paul and saw that he was tied similarly.

"What the hell?" she muttered before noticing the woman sitting in the chair at the foot of the bed.

"Sorry about this," said Sara. "I needed to be sure I could trust you two. No harm will come to you."

"Who are you?" asked Amy as she stared at the woman's face and then the flash of recognition came to her.

"Ah, I guess you know who I am by that expression," said Sara.

"You're a fucking killer!"

"Among other things. I'm not here to kill anyone though. I'm here to help you."

"By drugging us, and tying us up?"

"That's for both of our protection. Something is going on that you should know about."

"Paul!" shouted Amy, but he remained unconscious. "Is he okay?"

"He got a slighter larger dose of sedative. He also didn't get the antidote that you did. He'll be fine. It's you I needed to talk to."

"Why?"

"Rumor has it you're principled and a good investigator. You're said to be dedicated to your job. I've stumbled upon something rather big that needs to be investigated and prosecuted. It'll take a ballsy agent to take this on. I've been told you're just the person for the job."

Amy found her curiosity piqued and asked, "What did you find?"

"Some powerful people in the government are planning a coup," said Sara. She then reached down and removed a large stack of papers and set them on the bed. "These are electronic intercepts from the three main conspirators detailing their plan and agenda."

"Where did you get that?"

"A reliable source."

"Who are the plotters?"

"Senator Leeds, Shelby Johnson, and George Strauss."

"Seriously? You want me to take on arguably the three most powerful people in DC?"

"I said you'd need to be ballsy."

"Suicidal more like it," said Amy.

"Give it a read and follow your conscience," said Sara. "I suspect you'll do the right thing. I'll leave it all here, but for now, you've got to go back to sleep for a bit while I clear out."

Amy watched as Sar injected her with a syringe then all went black.

When Amy next awoke it was nearly an hour later. The files were still on the bed and both she and Paul had been cut free. Paul was still soundly asleep but seemed unharmed. Amy took her gun from the bedside table and checked the apartment, but Sara was long gone.

She went back into the bedroom and started to read through the files Sara had left and was still reading them when Paul finally woke up several hours later.

"God, did I sleep well last night," said Paul as he stretched.

"You missed the fun," said Amy looking up from the files. "We had a guest."

"Who?"

"Who's the most wanted woman in the world?"

"You know I've always had a thing for Selena Gomez."

"Thanks for reminding me, but no, not wanted in that way, but wanted criminally."

"Shit! Sara?"

"Bingo! She was here and left me these files. She'd drugged us both but woke me up and let you sleep through the whole thing."

"Why didn't you arrest her?"

"The whole arms tied together and secured to the headboard thing kind of slowed me down a bit. She wasn't here to cause us any trouble anyway, she was here just to give me these files."

"What are they?"

"Electronic intercepts, likely from one of the Five Eyes partners, showing a coup being planned by three of the most powerful people in DC. It's pretty impressive stuff. They want Schwartz out of office and replaced with Shelby Johnson. They might just be able to pull it off."

"Who are the three?"

"Strauss, Shelby Johnson, and Senator Leeds."

"Fuck!"

"Their plan might just work too."

"How the fuck did she get this stuff?" asked Paul as he started to leaf through a few of the documents.

"It appears she has friends in high places. This stuff is pretty inflammatory, I'm just not sure what I can do with it. The existing DOJ is allied with the three of them and won't move on them in the short time they have left in power. I have no idea who Schwartz will appoint as the new Attorney General, but I doubt they'd have the balls to go after those three."

"It's not balls as much as stupidity," muttered Paul still glancing through the documents.

"What do you mean?"

"Going after those three is suicide. They're the most powerful trio in DC. It's far better to have them on your side than against you. You'd have to be suicidal to try and hold them accountable for any of this. None of this is even likely admissible if it came through Five Eyes."

"But it opens the door for a real investigation where we could uncover real evidence that could be used against them."

"You're dreaming. You'd never be able to get charges to stick on any of these three. You saw the evidence against Shelby, hell, they had her confessing to crimes on videotape, and she walked free and is hailed as a hero by her followers."

"We can't sit back and do nothing. Sara brought these to me for a reason."

"Yeah, to destroy your career."

"No, I didn't get that vibe from her. She wanted me to bring these three down. She wanted to see justice done."

"She played the Wonder Woman game on you."

"The what?"

"The Wonder Woman game. It's how those close to you manipulate you. 'Oh, Amy, only you can help me.' It's how everyone who knows you gets you to do their work for them. Hell, George had you doing his filing for him the other day by playing that game."

"George is an idiot who doesn't know the alphabet, and if I'd left the filing up to him we'd never find those files again."

"He may be an idiot, but he knew how to manipulate you into doing his job. Sara's far from an idiot. She wants those three taken down and has decided to recruit you to do it. All you'll do is commit career suicide by working with her."

"What do you suggest then? We let the coup go unchallenged?"

"Honestly, we should use this to our tactical advantage. If those three want Schwartz removed from office, then he's out of office. They're that powerful. They don't know they're being monitored or they wouldn't be saying the stuff they're saying so openly. If we take this information to them and let them know what's going on, we'd become valuable to them. They'd owe us. When they took power, they'd likely reward us. I know you've got friends in the Schwartz campaign, but Schwartz is likely only in power for a few weeks, or months at most and then all his people will be swept aside. You can be swept aside and replaced at the drop of a hat. If we position ourselves on the other side, however, we'd be in a much better position going forward."

"You want me to ignore a coup?"

"I want you and us to survive. You can't use what you've got to get a warrant or open a real investigation. The current DOJ would shut you down in a heartbeat. I don't know what Schwartz's DOJ will be like, but I'm betting it won't be that different from the rest. How would you gather evidence against them that could be used in court?"

"I'll find some way."

"Because you think you're Wonder Woman. You're not. You're just Amy Jeter, a dedicated and beautiful FBI agent who thinks she can change the world. You can't beat those three. You can either join them and advance or get trampled to death by them. No one above you will support you in this and you can't do it alone. Sara was just trying to use you to get you killed. What she gave you though can be used to advance your career, hell, our careers. If we take this to Strauss and the rest and let them know they're being monitored and how they're doing it, they'll owe us."

"Blackmail? Seriously?"

"No, not blackmail," said Paul. "Just a little quid pro quo. We tell him, look, we found this out and we thought you should know what's going on. He'll be indebted to us and pay us back when his side's in power again. And they will be in power again."

"I can't be a part of that."

"You don't have to be. Just leave it to me but forget about pursuing this. It'll just lead to trouble. Let me handle everything."

CHAPTER THREE

Paul's meeting with Strauss was soon arranged and Paul informed Strauss of the news that he was being monitored and how it was being done. He turned over the documents Sara had left with Amy and was assured his efforts would not be forgotten. After he left a meeting was arranged with Shelby, Leeds, and Strauss at a secure location. There Strauss informed the other two of the situation.

"Sara's cooperating with the FBI?" muttered Shelby angrily.

"Just one agent, who is expendable," reassured Strauss. "Nothing they've gotten is usable in court and could only pose a PR danger. We can avoid even that by acting quickly. The agent who came to see me insisted they hadn't copied the documents and he surrendered the only copies they have. I doubt that's true, but we'll find out the truth of that soon enough."

"They're monitoring all three of us?" asked Leeds coldly.

"The NSA monitors everyone. This Sara person, who I'm beginning to develop an intense dislike for, has somehow managed to convince one of the Five Eyes partners to ferret through that data and forward the relevant stuff to her and from her to the FBI agent she's picked out. I've got sources inside the NSA who are looking to find the source there and end it. There's a very limited pool of possible suspects, so that shouldn't take long."

"So, what do we do in the meantime?" asked Leeds.

"We eliminate the threat," said Strauss. "There are just three people outside of the Five Eyes alliance who know what we're plotting, Sara and her two FBI agent friends. Sara may be very good at hiding, but her two friends aren't. We take them out and make sure no copies of the data they had still exist, then we continue our hunt for this Sara creature and find her and destroy her."

"The FBI agents could be dealt with by a couple of guys on my security team," said Leeds. "They're a hundred percent loyal to me and damned efficient at what they do."

"Excellent!" said Strauss. "Get them moving then. The sooner we get this resolved, the better."

* * *

Craig Burke got the message from his source inside the NSA and was alarmed. A visit had been arranged between one of the FBI agents who'd gotten the information from Sara and Strauss, then Strauss, Shelby, and Leeds had all gone quiet. The normally chatty threesome had gone quiet which meant they'd been tipped off to the surveillance. Craig Burke suspected they'd not want any witnesses to what they'd done kept around any longer than necessary.

He grabbed his coat and headed for his car. He needed to get a message to Charlie to try to get word to Sara about what was going on. Getting in to see Charlie took some talking, but finally, he was in. He handed Charlie a note he'd written and watched as Charlie frowned.

"I'll take care of this," said Charlie. "I just hope it's not too late." When Craig Burke left, Charlie penned a note of his own and whistled for Marley to come. As he pet the big dog around the head he slipped the note under the collar.

"Want to go for a walk big fella?" asked Charlie and Marley wagged his tail.

* * *

Amy had not been thrilled with Paul's plan, and had been a bit cross with him, but a night of his teasing her, caressing her, cuddling her, and love-making had eased her mind a bit.

"I guess it's not so bad," thought Amy. "The odds of holding those three accountable was largely insurmountable and maybe this would pay off in the end."

She looked over at Paul as he lay in bed, sound asleep as usual after their love-making, and smiled.

"Maybe I am Wonder Woman, but my superpower is to drain Paul of all his energy."

She, on the other hand, felt more awake than ever and knew it would be hours before she'd sleep. She decided a long hot shower was just the thing she needed, and she rose naked from the bed and walked into the bathroom closing the door behind her. The heat of the shower and the water washing over her body helped to take the stress and strain from her. As she was finishing the shower she thought she heard a noise from outside, but the roar of the pulsating showerhead made it unclear. She turned off the shower and listened but heard nothing. Still, she wrapped a towel around her body and headed out to check on the noise she'd heard. As she opened the bathroom door, two arms grabbed her arms and pinned them behind her back. She struggled to get free, but the person holding her was very strong and aware of her likely countermoves. Facing her was another man, holding her handgun that had been on her night table.

"Thanks for leaving this in plain sight," said the man leering at her. "It made the job much easier." He nodded towards the bed and Amy looked and saw two bullets holes in Paul's forehead as his eyes now looked emptily into space.

"No!" screamed Amy.

The man holding her gun had stepped forward and as she screamed he placed the barrel of the gun into her mouth choking off further protests. With his free hand, he undid the towel and let it slide to the floor.

"Very nice, very nice indeed," said the man as his eyes slid up and down her body. "Pity we had to make as much noise as we did, or we could have hung around and had some fun with you. As it is, we've got to get moving pretty soon."

His empty hand squeezed one of her breasts hard and then slid down her abdomen and into her vagina as she squirmed. He removed his fingers and gave them a sniff before smiling at Amy and saying, "Yeah, it's a damned shame. We could have had some fun with you. Oh well, maybe in another life. On your knees."

The man behind her holding her arms shoved against the back of her knees with his leg forcing them to buckle and Amy landed hard on her knees. With the gun still in her mouth and her arms pinned behind her, there was little she could do to resist.

"She's a lefty," said the man holding the gun, "so give me her left arm."

He saw the look of surprise on Amy's face and said, "I know you're a lefty as it took us three tries to find someone who could match your handwriting for the suicide note. It needed to be another lefty. And yes, you're committing suicide after murdering your lover after discovering he had an illicit affair with someone else. It'll be an open and shut case I'm afraid. Your gun fired all three shots and only your gun. No signs of forced entry thanks to our bump key. No signs of open resistance or a struggle. Just two dead lovers who'd had a spat. It happens all the time, especially among law enforcement officers."

Amy's left hand was dragged forward and passed to the man holding her gun in his mouth. She forced her hand into a fist and tried to resist opening it, but the man was very strong and squeezed hard enough to force her fingers open. He then threaded her trigger finger into place and Amy stared up at his face as she could feel him tightening the pressure on her finger.

The sound of the gunshot and the spray of blood wasn't a surprise when it came. Amy assumed she'd been shot. Only when the grip on her hand relaxed and the man's body fell atop of her, did she realize something else had happened. The second and third gunshots reinforced that belief. Amy was pinned under the man who'd been trying to kill her and looked to her left hand and saw the gun still there. She threw it aside and tried to move the man off her. A woman's hand grabbed the man's body by the shoulder and helped her roll his body aside.

Amy stared at Sara in shock and disbelief.

"Come on!" said Sara. "We haven't much time. You've got to get dressed and get out of here."

Amy was in a state of shock. Her lover lay dead on the bed. Two men lay dead on her bedroom floor, and the most wanted woman in the world was standing before her, holding a gun after saving her life.

"What the hell is going on?"

"We've got to get you out of here," said Sara. "Those men work for Leeds. I was barely able to get here in time to save you. I was too late for him," she added nodding towards Paul. "Leed's got more people in the area, so we've got to get going."

Amy largely stood frozen in place looking around the room.

Sara grabbed the clothes Amy had been wearing earlier that night from the bedside chair and tossed them to her.

"Get dressed, now. We've got to get going."

Amy nodded her head in agreement as she quickly pulled on the clothes she'd just taken off an hour or so earlier.

"They killed him," muttered Amy looking towards Paul's body on the bed.

"And they were about to kill you," reminded Sara as she picked up Amy's gun from where Amy had tossed it. "Do you have spare clips and ammo?" asked Sara.

Amy nodded to the wardrobe. Sara opened the doors and found what she needed. She put a fresh fully loaded clip into Amy's gun and then grabbed a couple of spares.

Amy was just finishing getting dressed when Sara walked over to her and handed her the gun and spare clips.

"You trust me with a gun?"

"Long term, no, short term, yes. We have mutual enemies nearby and lots of them. If they've figured out what we've done, we'll need all the firepower we can muster. God willing, we'll slip out before they catch on, but we can't count on luck. We need to be ready to fight our way out. Are you ready?"

Amy merely nodded, and Sara took her by the arm and led her to the door. A quick look down the hallway showed nothing unusual, so Sara led the way towards the fire stairs and cracked them open looking for any surprises, but no one was there.

"They're watching both the front and back doors," said Sara. "But they don't know the fire stairs dump into the alley. It's how I got in without a fight. Alley's aren't the best place to get caught however, so if things go bad, start shooting and don't stop, understand?"

Amy nodded, and Sara led her to the alley door. She cracked it open to check one direction, but the other way was blind. She stepped out into the alley and checked the other direction, ready to unleash a hail of bullets if need be, but no one was in sight. She motioned for Amy to join her.

"Okay, we're two drunk girls on our way home from a party now," said Sara mussing up Amy's hair and flipping up the collar on her blouse. You lean on me and I'll lean on you as we leave the alley. We'll turn left and stagger down the street to the corner. Once around the corner we can drop the pretense and take off, but there are too many people watching the immediate area to just run from the start. Keep your gun handy, but out of sight."

Amy nodded her head, tucked the gun into her waistband and the pair staggered out of the alley and off to the left. Amy took a glance around and noticed the two dark blue sedans parked nearby with occupants in them. She turned back and leaned heavily on Sara as though about to fall and whispered in her ear, "There are two dark blue sedans with watchers out front."

"There are two more out in the back," added Sara. "They won't be watching for long. When their triggermen don't return, they'll go looking for them and won't be happy with what they find."

"We could take them out," muttered Amy angrily, eager to avenge Paul's death.

"Too risky. We know there are eight of them and only two of us. The odds aren't in our favor for a fight here and now. We'll get them, just later. For now, we've just got to get away to someplace safe. We can get vengeance later."

They'd now reached the corner and staggered around it. Both took a second to look around and as they continued the stagger, but the coast was now clear.

"Fuck!" muttered Amy as she stood upright and backed away from Sara. "They killed him! They fucking killed him!"

"And they were going to kill you and blame both of your deaths on you. Here's the suicide note by the way. I thought you might want to keep it."

Amy read the note and was even more ready to kill someone after reading it. She had to admire the workmanship though. The writing was indistinguishable from her own. Authorities finding the note and the two bodies, all shot with Amy's gun, would quickly assume it was a murder-suicide.

"Do you know who did this?" asked Amy.

"Those guys were part of Senator Leeds security detail. Former Special Forces guys forced out of the military due to inappropriate conduct and recruited by him for his staff to deal with issues like you and Paul. He's got about ten of them. Well, had about ten of them. Now there's the eight that are left. Leeds no doubt gave them the final orders, but I dare say all three of the big three were involved in the decision-making process. Paul going to Strauss just made the two of you a big threat. You both knew stuff he didn't want made public, so he tried to have you killed to keep you silent."

"I'm not staying silent now. Thanks for saving me, by the way. And, believe me, you have no idea how weird it feels thanking someone like you."

"I almost didn't make it in time. Our side figured out what was happening, but we're forced to communicate in a somewhat awkward manner these days. By the time I got the word on what was happening, it was almost too late."

"You had like a second to spare. He was tightening my finger on the trigger when you shot him. I honestly thought I'd been shot until he fell on top of me."

"You're going to need to lie low for a while until I figure out a way to end all of this," said Sara. "Do you have a safe place to lie low?"

"No, I just have my apartment. Besides, I want in on ending all of this. I want those bastards dead for what they've done to me, for what they've done to Paul."

"It's probably best you just lie low for a while. I've got a safe house nearby I can stash you where you'll be safe. I'm not sure how much help you can be to me. You're too used to being on the good side of the law. I tend to be on the other side much of the time."

"I can help you. I'm one hell of an investigator and I can help you. I want these people dead more than you do. We'd make a hell of a team."

"We'll see," said Sara. "Step one is getting you off the streets and someplace safe. I could use some downtime myself. It's been a long day."

"I'm not sure I'll ever sleep again," muttered Amy.

"You will. Not well for a while, but eventually the sleep will come."

Sara led her away and towards her safe house.

* * *

"What the fuck happened?" demanded Leeds of the remainder of his team.

"We don't know," acknowledged the highest-ranking survivor of the operation. "Our guys went in, offed the guy, apparently found the girl in the shower. Her wet towel was on the bedroom floor. I guess she disarmed them somehow and shot them."

"They were shot by a different gun," reminded Leeds. "Gregor was shot in the back. Are you suggesting she escaped two highly trained, fit operatives, got a second gun, sneaked behind him and shot him?"

"It fits."

"No," said Leeds. "There had to be someone else there. Some bitch who just can't keep her nose out of our business. Fucking Sara! I'm sure it was her."

"We'd have seen her coming or going. We had both the back and front covered."

"So, where's the FBI agent then if you had everything covered?"

"We don't know."

"Did you see anyone at all in the area, or were you sleeping?"

"We weren't sleeping. There just wasn't anyone else around. There were a couple of drunk girls who came out of the alley after leaving a party and staggered off, but that's it."

Leeds let out a long sigh before responding.

"A couple of drunk girls? Seriously? You let them slip by you! Damn it! Am I the only one here with a fucking brain?"

"To be fair, we thought the girl was dead by then. We'd heard the shots and were just waiting for our team to return. As much as anything we were watching to be sure no law enforcement showed up prematurely. A couple of drunk girls at that hour of the night's not unusual."

"We fucking had them and let them slip away," muttered Leeds.

* * *

"In the news tonight," said the breathless anchor on the late news program playing in Sara's safe house, "a respected FBI agent is now on the run from authorities after shooting her lover and two people who heard the shots and tried to intervene. FBI Special Agent Amy Jeter is the prime suspect in the murder of the three men. Police and the FBI have launched a manhunt for Ms. Jeter and expect to have her in custody shortly. Anyone with information on her whereabouts is asked to call the FBI or their local police immediately. She is armed and considered extremely dangerous."

"But the other two weren't shot with my gun!" shouted Amy at the television. "My gun was in my mouth!"

"No," said Sara. "But ballistics reports are pretty easily faked if the people in charge want them faked. If those behind the shooting say it was your gun that shot all three men, then that's what the early reports will say. The reports may change down the road, but for the foreseeable future, it'll be your gun that shot the three."

"I'm so fucked."

"No, you're not. We'll get you through this. It's just going to take some time."

"A whole fucking lifetime. All I've worked for my whole life is gone. My best friend n the world is dead. My whole reputation is gone. As far as the world is concerned I'm a fucking psycho killer bitch like you now. No offense."

"Have you ever killed anyone?" asked Sara.

"No," said Amy.

"Then you're not a psycho fucking killer bitch like me. You're Amy Jeter, FBI agent, and discoverer of the truth. You know a hell of a lot more of what's going down than all but a handful of people.

"And there's not a fucking thing I can do about it. Paul's dead. I'm ruined and I'm taking advice from you. This is not how I saw my life going."

"The good news is the two guys who killed Paul are now dead and facing an eternity of whatever waits for them on the other side. My guess is it won't be pleasant. We know who gave the orders. We just have to find a way to hold them accountable."

"As much as it pains me to say this, Paul was right. We'll never be able to hold them accountable. They're too powerful and too corrupt to topple. Even you've failed in toppling Shelby and you never fail. I can't even go out in public without people recognizing me and sounding the alarm."

"Ah, that's where you're wrong," said Sara. "Step this way."

Sara led her to a large cabinet and swung open the two full-length doors to reveal her stash.

"There's enough hair coloring in here to open several salons. There are wigs, hair extensions in every color, colored contact lenses, fake tattoos, and every type of makeup imaginable. I've got a variety of prosthetic ears, noses, cheekbone and chin enhancements that can be glued onto your existing features to change them. Careful application, some matching foundation and you can look completely different. There's a room that's filled with nothing but clothes that can change your appearance dramatically. From this safe house, you can emerge as an eighty-year-old woman or a young goth woman. There's nothing about your appearance we can't change. I've got shoes here with up to a ten-inch platform if you need to be taller and we've got flats. They won't make you any shorter, but they won't make you appear taller. I can knock five to ten years of age off you or make you sixty or seventy years older if need be.

"One of the things you'll discover is that most people don't pay attention to other people. You do because you've been trained to, but to most, you'll just be a face in the crowd and not a wanted woman. Trust me, I know. Give me an hour or two and your mother won't recognize you."

"Seriously? That's how you've stayed free for so long?"

"I hardly use any of it anymore. Like I said, you just blend into the crowd in most places and most times. If I'm heading someplace where I'm likely to be recognized, I'll take the extra precautions, but most of the time I just go as myself and no one notices me.

"When you first saw me at the foot of your bed, did you immediately recognize me?"

"No, it took a few seconds. I knew I'd seen your face, but it took me a blink or two to figure out where."

"And you're a trained observer. Most people will think I'm someone they went to school with, saw on TV, saw a picture of, but they don't associate my face with being a killer's face. I smile, I treat people nice. They don't expect that from a killer, so they don't link me to being Sara the, what were the words you used, fucking psycho killer bitch? They may even think I bear a resemblance to her, but I can't be a killer because I'm so nice. You'll see. You won't be noticed."

"I'm not you though."

"Keep watching the news and see the photos they use identifying you. Note the hair color, style, length, where you part your hair, see how you're clothed in the photos. Watch for your makeup. All of that can be changed. I'll tweak your appearance tomorrow and take you out for a test run and you'll see what I mean. No one, and I mean no one, will recognize you."

"But, that still doesn't solve the problem of the big three. How do we go after them?"

"Divide and conquer. That all starts tomorrow, and we play no role initially. Our allies will handle that stage for now."

"Our allies?"

"We're not in this fight alone. For once in my life, I'm part of a team with a common goal. And that goal is taking down those three."

"And we're supposed to just sit here while your supposed teammates have all the fun?"

"No. We'll take you out for a walk in the park tomorrow in disguise to see how well we can pull that off and if anyone recognizes you."

"Seriously?"

"Do you have something better to do?"

"No, I guess not."

* * *

Benjamin and Charlie were meeting with their transition team to go over more appointments. After multiple smaller roles get filled, the discussion moved to the Secretary of State.

"I thought we had that down to two names," said one of the team members.

"I'm adding a third name," said Benjamin. "What about Senator Leeds?"

"That douchebag?" asked the same team member.

"He's a member of the party in good standing. Should disaster befall us, he'd be in the line of secession to carry on our work."

"I think he might be a good pick for your side," said Charlie. "It could help to keep the party behind us. God knows we're planning to do some things that will rattle both parties, so having someone like him on our team could help."

"I'm assuming the background check won't be a problem," said Benjamin.

"Senator Douchebag could write it himself," muttered the disgruntled aide. "He's got that kind of power in this city. I thought we were coming to town to change things. To shake up the establishment. There's no one more establishment than Senator Douchebag."

"Sometimes having the establishment on your side could be a good thing," said Charlie.

"Indeed," said Benjamin. "From what I understand he was to be Shelby's VP if she'd won the nomination. I considered him for the job myself before opting for Charlie. Having a smart, principled man like Senator Leeds on our side could be a very good thing."

* * *

Sara spent nearly an hour the next morning altering Amy's appearance, keeping Amy facing away from the mirror while she worked. Sara stood back one final time and then smiled and nodded for Amy to turn around and look at herself.

"Holy shit!" muttered Amy. "Is that me?"

Amy looked about twenty years older, ten pounds heavier in the face and neck thanks to the prostheses and was all but unrecognizable even to herself.

"It's you," said Sara. "Like I said, you can change your appearance, so no one will recognize you. I gave you some extra heft in your face and neck and I've got padded bodysuits that you could wear to achieve that same effect for your body. I can change you back to your old self, or into someone else in a few minutes also. Most of the clothes you'll find in my storeroom are reversible, so you can quickly change your look. With some practice, in five seconds of being out of sight, you can emerge dressed completely differently. I've got a few skirts with rolled-up pants legs hidden inside. Step out of the skirt, flip it inside out, undo the velcro holding the legs in place and step in and you've gone from wearing a skirt to pants in a blink."

"This is pretty darn amazing," mused Amy as she reached up to touch her face before pausing. "Can I touch it?"

"Sure. The glue for the prosthetic pieces holds pretty well and the pieces are contoured to blend in smoothly."

Amy touched her face and for the first time truly believed it was her. She made a series of faces to test the movement and couldn't believe the results.

"You're a fucking genius," said Amy.

"It's more experience than anything. I've been needing to do this sort of thing to survive for some time now. As you know, a whole lot of people are hunting me. I can't make it too easy for them. What do you say we take the new you out for a little walk in a nearby park after we get some clothes on you?"

A few minutes later Amy and Sara left the safe house and headed for the nearby park, but Amy suddenly tensed.

"What's up?" asked Sara.

"Something's wrong," said Amy. "We're being watched. Two men on the roof of the hotel on the left."

Sara nodded and replied, "There are two more on the roof of the restaurant to your right and two more in the silver sedan at the far end of the park. If it's any help there's another six men armed to the teeth in a van somewhere nearby."

"You knew?"

"They're good guys and on our side. For now anyway. They check to be sure I'm not being followed or bothered while I exchange information with a source."

Sara led a somewhat nervous Amy over to where Marley was tugging at the end of his leash anxious to reunite with Sara.

"I wasn't expecting company," said the team leader to Sara nodding to Amy as Sara greeted Marley.

"Bob, meet Amy Jeter. Most wanted woman in all of DC now, present company excluded of course."

"Whoa! Sorry if this comes off wrong, but you look much better in photos than real life. I'm assuming that's Sara's handiwork?"

"What do you think of it? Is it good enough to fool anyone?" inquired Sara.

"Fucking everyone. My guys on the radio had no clue who she was, and her picture's been all over the news." He then turned to Amy and said, "I'm assuming you're on our side then?"

"I don't know which side that is, I just know which side I'm not on and that's the Leeds, Strauss, Johnson side. Not after what they did to me."

"That pretty much puts you on our side then," said Bob.

Sara was busy nuzzling Marley during this conversation and then removed the message from Charlie and added one of her own to Marley's collar.

"We'd best be getting out of here," said Sara. "I thought I'd give the new Amy a bit of a test run to see how she fared in disguise."

"You did good. Hell, even knowing who she is, I wouldn't recognize her."

"Take care of the pup," said Sara as she gave Marley one final pet then ushered Amy out of the park.

"So, friends of yours then? You don't always operate alone?"

"Everyone needs a few good friends," said Sara.

"And the dog's a carrier pigeon of some sort."

"See, you are a good investigator. He's an old friend. With all electronic communication being intercepted and rooms bugged there was a need to find a new way to share information."

"And the guys watching the park?"

"Colleagues who want to make sure we're not interrupted or disturbed. They're damned good at what they do. If things had gone wrong back there, all hell would have broken loose."

"What message did you send or receive?"

"I sent a message saying you were safe and with me. I got a message that our operation divide and conquer was underway."

"There's no way you're going to divide those three. They're tied together too closely."

"Egos are powerful and fragile things. There are three enormous egos involved. A bit of careful tweaking can bring about some great rewards."

* * *

"Something came up that I wasn't expecting," mused Strauss at the next meeting of the three. "Something that may no longer make it necessary to have that special election with all of the complications it would bring."

"What happened?" asked Shelby.

"It turns out our two newly elected leaders, Tweedle-dumb and Tweedle-dumber, are now considering Senator Leeds here for the job of Secretary of State. That would put him in the line of secession. If we could take out those ahead of him in line, the Speaker could step aside and he'd earn the presidency legitimately, and we wouldn't have to trust the will of the fickle voters."

"But, where does that leave me?" asked Shelby.

"You could take over at State, or maybe the VP under Leeds if we could arrange that. Let the two morons hold the office for a couple of weeks, hell maybe for two full years, impeach them, insert Leeds so he could hold two additional full terms and then rotate you in after that Shelby. It could be eighteen years of uninterrupted power if we managed it properly."

"But we'd leave the morons in charge for two full years?"

"They won't be able to do much harm in that time."

"Easy for you to say as you'd left before Schwartz got the records from the Hasselberg Group. Benjamin Schwartz will use those two years to torture me and those of us in the group. He's still got that stolen data and his AG could very well be hostile to the group."

"With Leeds as part of the Cabinet, he could help steer things in other directions, isn't that right Senator?"

Senator Leeds was a bit lost and didn't initially hear the question as he was busy imagining the things he could accomplish over ten years as unquestioned leader of the free world. When the question was repeated to him he assured Shelby he'd do everything in his power to deflect the heat from her and her former allies if he was in the Cabinet.

"I don't like this plan," muttered Shelby. "It's too risky."

It wasn't so much the risk that bothered her as the thought of not being in power for at least ten full years. She craved the power of the presidency like a starving man craves a meal. Knowing she'd have to wait eight years after the election of those two morons was bad, but the plan to topple them and force a special election with days or weeks had sounded great. Now, that plan was in danger of being shelved for one where she'd have to wait ten full years for another shot at the office.

"Think about the upside," said Strauss. "Eighteen years of unfettered power to do whatever we choose!"

"We can't guarantee those eighteen years though," said Shelby. "Elections have to take place. Campaigns need to be run. As the voters have shown far too often, they'll vote however they damned well please. We can't guarantee they'll vote our way. Hell, Leeds could be out of power after just two years if we do it this way, and you're giving the two morons two full years to do whatever they want. I just don't see the upside of this method when we get flush them sooner and install me in their place. God willing, by the end of January I could be president and we'd have more power than before if we stuck to the original plan. With Leeds as my VP, he'd be poised to step in eight years from now, and we could have someone else poised to step in when those eight years were done."

"I understand your viewpoint Shelby," said Strauss. "But we're going to see if we can't get Leeds the State job and go from there. Our efforts to entrap this Sara creature have gone nowhere and that makes calling for the special election nearly impossible. At this time, I think it's the best option and there's no more need for discussion."

* * *

After returning to Sara's apartment and getting some lunch Amy asked what else was planned.

"I need to do some recon work," said Sara. "You can stay here if you want, or come along with me. It's up to you."

"Where are you going?"

"My latest satellite photos of Shelby's mansion has some new structures on it that puzzle me. I've been to her place before and there's new stuff there that I want to know more about."

"Are you going to kill her?"

"If need be, but not just yet. With any luck, their power trio will implode on its own and they may even take each other out. Enemies of Shelby's have a habit of dying prematurely. She might just take out Leeds and Strauss for us."

"So, when do we leave?" asked Amy.

* * *

Shelby returned to her Connecticut mansion in a foul mood.

"How dare that son of a bitch steal the presidency from me!" screamed Shelby as she vented her rage to her assistant Herman. "This was all set up for me to assume the office, not that asshole. He was to be the VP. Now they want me to wait ten years? Ten fucking years! Are they out of their fucking minds?"

"To hell with them," said Herman. "You don't need them."

"I do need them though," muttered Shelby. "Winning an election without Strauss's support in the party is nearly impossible. He's like a goddamn god and he knows it. Leeds isn't far behind him. Those two fuckers have made a side deal between themselves and I'm left on the outside."

"So, go after Leeds and knock him down. Make him a bad choice for the job. If he doesn't get Secretary of State and isn't in the line of secession, then they have to go back to the original plan."

"How do I target Leeds?" asked Shelby.

"He's politically vulnerable. Don't forget he's had one aide participate in a murder-suicide and two of his security guys got shot when they'd have a hard time explaining why they were even in the area. The story that they heard the gunshots and heroically rushed in to save the day only to get shot and killed, just doesn't add up. They didn't live remotely near to the place. What were they doing there? Why did they hear the gunshots when nearby residents didn't? How did they get in? An FBI agent in an iffy neighborhood just leaves her door unlocked? My police source tells me they found an assortment of bump keys on one of the guys. Those aren't something normal people carry around with them. The real ballistics tests on the bullets show they came from two different guns."

"Wait? The real ballistics tests?"

"I've got a source in the DC police. The results that have been made public aren't accurate. The story Leeds and his media allies have painted is one very sympathetic to him. We have our media allies also though and we can paint a much darker picture. One where his two thugs break into the apartment for some reason, find the agent's gun, shoot her boyfriend then she appears, confronts them with a different gun, shoots them both and escapes, fleeing for her life. A well-placed rumor or two that she was investigating Senator Leeds and he goes from sympathetic victim to a madman intent of preventing his crimes from being uncovered. It's not a tough spin job. There are things he's done with foreign aid and his foundation that could be leaked that would destroy any chance he has of being Secretary of State."

"I like the way you think my boy. You've just brightened up my whole day. If he doesn't get the Secretary of State job, then we have to fall back on the old plan. Can you arrange those stories so they don't get traced back to us?"

"Our media allies will shield us from Leeds, you don't have to worry about that. They consider him something of an asshole. The ballistics reports and police report on the bump keys will support our narrative. Leeds will have to withdraw as a candidate or Schwartz will drop him. Having a murderer and two psychopathic killers on your team makes him a bad option for Secretary of State."

CHAPTER FOUR

The trip to Shelby's Connecticut mansion took the better part of four hours with Sara driving the whole time. Amy found herself annoyed by pretty much everything lately and was feeling a bit peevish on the trip.

"You do know that even though the speed limit is just sixty-five, you can speed a little?" asked Amy as they neared the small town where the mansion was situated.

"Right now, we're two of the most wanted people on the planet. It's best not to draw undue attention to ourselves if possible. Lots of criminals get caught by doing something stupid. I'll occasionally do something stupid, but so far, I've been lucky. I try not to push that luck too hard."

Sara drove past Shelby's mansion with the huge iron gates and iron fencing surrounding it as Amy looked out. The guardhouse with two of Shelby's Russian bodyguards inside it caught her attention the most.

"So," asked Amy. "What are we looking for?"

"The new stuff I've seen is around the back of the property. There's an old dirt road not too far ahead where I can park the car and then we can hike through the woods behind the property to get a look."

Sara soon had the car parked and two had worked their way through the woods, so they could see the back of Shelby's house and the structures now between the back of the house and the fence that encircled the property. The mystery of the new structures was soon revealed. They were dog houses and chained to the front of each house was a large black dog that looked to be in a bad mood. Two of them were staring each other down and then lunging towards one another barking only to be brought up a foot short of each other by the chains that secured them to the dog houses.

"I think I know those dogs," said Amy.

"How?"

"I worked undercover with the Russian mob in New York City. One of the guys in the mob was always bragging about this new breed of dog he was creating. They were part Mastiff, part Pit Bull, part Rottweiler, and part Russian wolf. He was breeding them to be the ultimate fighting dog. He'd bring one with him from time to time, but he'd have to keep it muzzled. He'd trained them to fight and attack anything if they heard the right word and he couldn't be sure they wouldn't hear the word when he didn't want them attacking someone. He'd show us how they responded to the command with the muzzle on and it was scary as hell. He trained them in Russian and they could be good obedience trained dogs most of the time."

"And you think that's them?"

"It looks like them. I can find out though. Give me a lift over the fence."

"Seriously?"

"Their chains don't reach this far. You can see how far they can come. I expect them to charge me but be pulled up short. If I'm right I can then give them some commands and we'll see what they do."

"You speak Russian then?"

"Like I said, I was undercover with the Russian mob. I had to know Russian. I have a bit of a Brooklyn accent to my Russian but that didn't matter in New York. We'll see if it matters to these guys."

Sara gave Amy a boost up the fence and the two nearest dogs sprang forward snarling and baring their teeth and barking furiously as Amy neared them.

"Tikho!" said Amy firmly and the two dogs stopped barking and looked at her quizzically.

"Sidet'!" commanded Amy. Both dogs sat. Amy stepped forward into the range of the first dog and scratched his head as she cooed, "Khoroshaya sobaka." The dog sat there wagging his tail as she pet his head. He was soon lying on his back wagging his tail as she rubbed his belly. The second of the dogs was now whining and begging for attention and Amy went to him and gave him some attention before stopping and retreating to the fence where Sara reached through and helped her back over.

"I wouldn't have believed that if I didn't see it myself," said Sara.

"Like I said, I know those guys. Well, probably their parents or grandparents now. It's been a few years. They're still trained the same way though. They still follow the same commands. They're nice dogs if you know how to talk to them. You just have to be careful what you say."

"I may just have to learn some Russian dog commands," said Sara.

"Or have someone with you who already knows them. I'm thinking we could be a good team."

"Could be. Let's take a look at that guard station out front while we're here."

The two made their way through the edge of the woods to where they could see the guard station. A heavy gate prevented any unwanted entry. There were two guards inside the station and two more in an addition that had been made to the front of the house.

"How many guards does she have?" asked Amy.

"Seven at the last count. There were a few more, but they had an unfortunate accident."

"Being sucked out of a plane at thirty-thousand feet is more than unfortunate. How'd you do that anyway?"

"That's a story for another day. What's this?"

A delivery van had just pulled up from a local food vendor and the two guards inside the station and the two others from inside now converged on the van. The final three guards also emerged from the house and joined the rest. They paid the driver and he removed a large insulated box from the back and passed out the food from the box. All four guards laughed with the driver then waved goodbye as he drove off. The guards sat nearby and gulped down the food and drinks before returning to their normal stations.

"All seven guards eat from one delivery van," mused Sara.

"You're thinking of drugging them?"

"It could be challenging. Intercepting the food and tampering with it without the driver noticing would be tricky. They know and like the driver and he seemed friendly enough with them."

"There might just be a way to do it," mused Amy. "How about we make a detour on our way back south?"

"Where to?" asked Sara.

"There's a little electronics place I know in NYC and a guy who runs it who could be a big help to us."

* * *

"How are things going?" asked Craig Burke as Charlie and he were meeting in the Bentley secure conference room.

"So far, so good," said Charlie. "We've got some things in motion that might just work out okay. I gather our three enemies have gone very quiet lately?"

"Yes. They're only meeting in person now or by courier and no more phone, texts, or emails, so our friends at the NSA are being shut out of their planning."

"We pretty much know what we need to know now anyway," said Charlie. If things work out right, we may just be able to split up the gruesome threesome and then settle matters.

* * *

"This is your electronics store?" asked Sara as Amy led her to the door of a rowhouse in a very dodgy part of the city.

"Store might have been a bit of an exaggeration," admitted Amy. "But this guy has something we could use."

She knocked on the door and then stared up at the lone security camera above the door.

"Get the hell out of here!" came a voice over the intercom.

"It's me, Pablo," said Amy. "Open the door or I'll knock it down."

"Amy?" asked a very confused voice. "You don't look like Amy."

"And you won't look like Pablo when I get done with you if you don't open the fucking door."

The electronic door lock could be heard to open and Amy led the way inside.

"Hey, Pablo!" said Amy. "How are you, my old friend?"

"What the fuck happened to you? I didn't recognize you."

"Things went a bit south in DC and I had to adopt a disguise."

"I'm more than a little surprised to see you here. Last I heard you were wanted by the FBI." Pablo placed a gun on the counter with his hand on the trigger and pointed it towards Amy.

"You know Paul was my friend," said Pablo. "They say you killed him."

"And he was my lover and if you think I had anything to do with his killing then kill me now. I like to think you know me better than that though."

Pablo looked at her eyes long and hard then nodded his head and placed the gun back behind the counter.

"I couldn't believe it when they said he'd been killed and you were the suspect," said Pablo.

"You can't believe anything you hear or see these days. I'd be dead too now if it wasn't for her," said Amy nodding towards Sara who was staying back a bit. "They were setting it up to look like a murder-suicide with me the killer. My gun was in my mouth and my hand forced on the trigger when my friend here showed up and took out the two guys who'd shot Paul and were planning to shoot me."

"Good timing," said Pablo.

"Not good enough to save Paul," said Sara.

"Shit happens," said Pablo.

"I need your help, Pablo," said Amy. "I need one of your spoofers."

"You know they're illegal," said Pablo.

"Yeah, well I don't give a damn right now. I just need one."

Pablo sighed and pulled out a device from a drawer and set it in front of her.

"Seriously?" asked Amy feigning disbelief. "I want a good one, not this cheap shit. I could get this from anyone. I need one of yours, Pablo. Not this mass-produced shit."

"These work fine," said Pablo.

"Bullshit!" muttered Amy. "If that's all you've got to offer me then I'm out of here. From what I hear Hector has a new place on the East Side."

"Hector? That hack?" muttered Pablo. "You'd go to him?"

"I need a good spoofer Pablo. I don't give a fuck who sells it to me. I don't want this cheap crap though."

"Alright, alright, you win," said Pablo pulling back the cheap spoofer from the counter. "I'd promised this one to someone else, but maybe I can get another put together before he comes to pick it up."

He produced a larger, more substantial device from under the counter.

Amy examined it closely then nodded her approval.

"How much?" asked Amy.

"For anyone else, ten grand. For you, five."

"I'll give you two."

"Two? Are you mad! It cost me more than that to make it!"

"Seriously?" asked Amy. "I know what this costs to make. You're making a lot at two grand."

"Come on, Amy. A man has to eat."

"I'm hoping to use this to nail Paul's killer," said Amy. "Think about that."

"That's not fair! You know I liked Paul."

"Two grand is my top offer," said Amy. She pulled her pistol out and held it by her side. "I'm walking out of here with this and you either get two grand, or you get shot. Those are the only two options."

"Fuck it! Paul never treated me like this!"

"Where do you think I learned to treat people like this?" asked Amy. "You know Paul would handle this the same way. You take the two grand or you're out of business in a very permanent fashion."

Pablo laughed a bit at that, remembering the time when Paul nearly strangled him to get a better price, then nodded his head.

"Two grand then," said Pablo. The money changed hands and then Amy picked up the device. Amy and Sara headed back to the car.

"That was a bit intense," said Sara.

"Typical for Pablo," said Amy.

"So, what exactly is a spoofer?"

"Cars are radio transmitters on wheels these days. They use radio to communicate with key fobs to know if you're around. That delivery truck driver has a key fob for the truck. Using this we can spoof the code on his fob and open the back of the truck whenever we'd like. We could use it to lock, unlock, start, or stop the truck if we wanted to. Once we get the right code, we'll pretty much own the truck."

"That could be handy."

"More than that, it could get us into Shelby's house despite her guards. We get the truck to stop on the way to make the delivery, I distract the driver while you pop in the back and drug the food. Then we wait until the sedatives take effect and visit dear old Shelby."

"And then?"

"Then we get revenge for what she and her friends did to Paul."

* * *

Senator Leeds was not a happy man.

"Where the hell did this story come from?" he screamed to Strauss. "I thought we had the press on a tight leash?"

"My media sources say a police source leaked the story to a receptive reporter and she got the story past her editor. It got picked up nationally before we could intervene. It should die down quickly though. They've reported all there is to report which is just the bump keys and ballistics reports. There's nothing there to directly implicate you in the deaths."

"And the story about the donations to my foundation? Where did that come from?"

"I'm still looking into that."

"It's going to make my selection as Secretary of State harder for Schwartz to justify, and the Republicans will make hay of it during the confirmation process. The timing couldn't be worse."

"Don't worry my boy. You being Secretary of State and taking over the presidency wasn't our only card to play. We can always go back to plan A."

"And have me as VP to Shelby? Yeah. Care to bet she had a hand in this whole thing?"

"I wouldn't rule it out," admitted Strauss. "Shelby desperately wants to be President and sitting out ten years would not be ideal for her."

"How the fuck am I supposed to work with her if she pulls this kind of bullshit?"

"Shelby should remember the old admonition that people who live in glass house shouldn't throw stones. She lives in a very fragile house and I have a lot of stones. We'll talk this out at our next full meeting and resolve any lingering issues. Just do as you're told for now and all will be okay."

"Do as you're told," muttered Leeds to himself as he drove away from the meeting. "He talks to me like I'm a fucking two-year-old. He should realize that Shelby isn't the only person living in a glass house and I've got a few stones of my own."

* * *

Benjamin and Charlie couldn't help but smile at one another as they discussed the implications of the news story about Senator Leeds.

"How does this affect the potential of Leeds as Secretary of State?" asked Charlie.

"It makes it harder to justify his nomination, that's for sure. It doesn't look good when three people that close to you are involved in murders in some capacity. That Dolph kid was close to him and then the two guys killed in the apartment by the FBI agent being part of his security detail looks bad. We can talk to him and see if he has an explanation as to why they were there, why they had bump keys, and what they were doing there, but if this story lingers, he's probably out."

"Pity, I think he'd have made a good Secretary of State. Any idea how the story got out?"

"I suspect an enemy of his spread the word. Rumors were circulating that we were offering him the Secretary of State job, or considering him for it, so someone didn't want him to have it. Welcome to DC. This is par for the course."

"The reporter who broke the story is from Connecticut isn't she?"

"Yeah, I believe so."

"Shelby Johnson might have been the source then."

"Could be. She's still pissed at not being nominated. Taking down a potential future rival wouldn't be beyond her. She tried to kill me, so spreading a few stories about Leeds wouldn't be out of the question."

"So, Leeds is a no go then?"

"Unless things change in a hurry. He needs to explain what's been happening in his office with his people. Three dead and all involved in a murder in some manner doesn't look good."

"Any word on if they've found that FBI agent yet?"

"Not yet. I'm starting to hear whispers that she's been investigating something big and that's why she was targeted."

"By Leeds?"

"Could be, or someone else, but the whispers I'm hearing are that she's still gathering information on the outside and will reappear when she's got everything she needs."

"Good for her."

* * *

Senator Leeds had called in his closest aide and the two were meeting outside where they couldn't be overheard or eavesdropped on.

"Find out what you can on who's behind leaking that damned story on me."

"I've already looked. From what I've seen, it comes from Connecticut and Shelby Johnson, or someone close to her."

"That fucking bitch!"

"She didn't want you as Secretary of State."

"We'll see about that. I've got to talk to those two morons and try to convince them to keep me in mind for the job. If they don't then a potential ten years of me in charge will be gone and I'll be Shelby's fucking puppet for the next eight years. I'm not going for that. If we can't get me in the line of secession, then I want me to be the choice for the nominee as the replacement instead of Shelby. I'll be damned if I'll serve under that lying bitch."

"We can poison her with some of our friends in the media."

"It's going to take a shitload of poison to kill her though," muttered Leeds. "She's been up to her eyeballs in filth the whole time and the idiot voters still rally around her."

"There are ways to pry them apart. She's said some things privately in fundraisers to friendly crowds that she doesn't want made public. I've heard the tapes and seen some videos. I've kept copies of most of them. We can leak those to our friends in the media and Shelby will lose a lot of her credibility."

"What's she said?"

"She's called black voters slaves for the party. She's insulted everyone who isn't a white, upper-class, Northeastern Democrat at one time or another. Her speech varies from group to group, but I've heard her attack Jews, Muslims, Blacks, Hispanics, whites, the poor, the middle class, and pretty much anyone who isn't represented in whatever fundraiser she's attending. She forgets that people can and do record things even when they're not supposed to. Those recordings exist. A few well-timed leaks of them will hurt her badly."

"Can you do it so it can't be traced back to me?"

"Sure."

"Then do it. She wants to play dirty, we'll see how low she wants to go."

"We could go even lower," suggested the aide.

"How low?"

"The body-cam footage of the sheriff when he arrested her is pretty damning. I've seen it."

"How the hell did you see it? They wouldn't even release it to Congress for our investigation."

"I know one of the deputies out there and he got me a copy of it. It's not good for Shelby. She claims she was disoriented and confused, but in the video, she's more boasting of her power and her ability to destroy anyone who gets in her way. She doesn't look disoriented or confused. She looks angry that anyone would try to stand up to her."

"And you still have that footage?"

"I sure do. I figured it might come in handy sometime. I've been kind of surprised it hasn't shown up on one or more of the anonymous file-sharing sites like

4chan, or the sort. I suppose it could be released there quite easily. Once it's out, it'll spread like wildfire."

"And it's damning?"

"Of both her and the idiots on the jury who acquitted her."

"Could it be traced back to you?"

"No. The deputy and I are old friends. As far as anyone knows he doesn't even have the video. He stole a copy from the sheriff for himself. Once he saw it he thought I should know about it."

"Let's light a little fire under dear old Shelby then."

"And what about Strauss?"

"Look up that legislation the Republicans proposed a few years back on limiting charitable write-offs to liberal groups. We defeated it, but I want a fresh look at it. We may just need to come out with a revised version of it."

"The Anti-Strauss bill?" asked the aide nervously. It had been nicknamed that as it targeted many of the groups and organizations he founded. "He won't be happy if he hears you're looking at that again."

"Fuck him! It's not like he's making my life any easier right now. He's treating me like a two-year-old who must obey his every command. I need to put the fear of God back into him. I'm not his fucking puppy to obey his every command. He's forgotten we're supposed to be partners and he's treating me like a servant. I'm no one's fucking servant."

"If that bill passes," mused the aide.

"It'll cost Strauss billions, force him to close most of those support groups, and open up the playing field to candidates who don't have to be in his back pocket to have a chance. Benjamin Schwartz was a big backer of that original bill. I can use my support of it as leverage to stay in the contention for the Secretary of State job. Schwartz wants to blow up DC and level the playing field, that's one way to do it. Strauss funnels billions through those groups to his favored candidates, and it's becoming clear to me that I'm not a favored candidate, so fuck him. We may not have to use it but having it ready as a threat is a good thing for us."

"Yes, Sir."

* * *

"I hate just sitting around and doing nothing," muttered Amy.

"There's lots of stuff is going on behind the scenes," reassured Sara. "We'll be getting a new intelligence dump later today if things play out right for you to sort through."

"None of which we can use to prosecute those who ordered Paul or my deaths. I already know who did what and why. I want Strauss's head on a plate followed by the other two."

"Everything in due time. We just have to be careful. Strauss is very powerful and dangerous to cross. We can take him down, but it'll take some time. His mansion is guarded like Fort Knox. Getting in is nearly impossible. He's reportedly got diffraction grating on the windows to keep snipers at bay. You aim where his image is, and he's not there, but a few feet away in a seemingly random direction. We need to be smart taking on a guy like him. We can't take a shot and miss. When we go after him, we have to be sure we get him."

"It just pisses me off knowing he's living a life of luxury while I'm holed up here hiding out. He's killed my best friend in the world and the man I was to marry, and he's walking around free as a bird. No one's even looking at him for ordering the killing. Hell, Leeds' two men were there and no one was even looking at Leeds until that newspaper story broke. Now it looks like that's already died down."

"They'll get theirs. It's just a question of time. We will win this fight."

"But, I'm still wanted for murder and I can't even work to clear my name. People think I killed Paul and the two guys who were there to kill us. I haven't killed anyone and everyone's looking for me while those responsible are free and happy. I don't even know how I'd clear my name after all of this. The real killers are dead. I'm guessing you won't testify on my behalf. The public's been fed the tail of me ambushing the two good Samaritans who rushed in to help Paul after I shot him, so the jury will be set against me. Who on the jury is going to believe that I was nearly one of the victims of a staged murder/suicide and you saved me?"

"We've got the intelligence reports showing them targeting you."

"That we can't use in court because they were gathered improperly."

"So, we get a confession from those involved."

"Like they'll volunteer to give us a confession. We can't even get anything legally now as they've figured out we're monitoring them after Paul gave them the heads up. They're very careful what they say and where they say it now. I'm just fucked! If I get caught I'll go to prison for the rest of my life for a crime I didn't commit."

"Then we can't have you getting caught."

"Everyone gets caught eventually. I'm not like you. I have friends, family I need to be in contact with. I can't be only exchanging notes through a fucking dog for the rest of my life. I need my old life back."

"That's going to be challenging."

"What if we made a deal of some sort?"

"What kind of deal?"

"I don't know. Give Strauss something he wants in exchange for him letting the word out that the two guys were the killers and I was an intended victim."

"There's nothing we have that he'd want enough to do that. He wants the presidency in the hands of one of his pawns. Short of selling out Benjamin and Charlie, which I won't do, there's nothing that we can offer."

"I know. It's just so frustrating being in this position."

"We'll get this taken care of. I promise you. You'll get back to your real-life somehow. Trust me."

"God, I hope so."

* * *

George Strauss was not a happy man as he paced the floor of his private study watching his two supposed allies glare at one another.

"Anyone care to explain to me what the hell is going on?" demanded Strauss.

"Someone's trying to sabotage me," said Senator Leeds nodding towards Shelby.

"Oh, that's just bullshit! I never said anything against you. It's more you who's trying to sabotage me! The body-cam footage? My private speeches, all getting released? You don't think I know who's behind that?"

"And you think I played a role in that?" asked Leeds feigning innocence. "I know that the story tying my office to the murders came from a reporter in your backyard. Did she just coincidentally develop a source in DC from Connecticut?"

"How the fuck do I know who her source is, but everything she printed was accurate, was it not?"

"Every bit as accurate as your body-cam footage and speech footage I would guess," retorted Senator Leeds.

"Enough of this!" shouted Strauss. "We're supposed to be a team. We're supposed to be working towards a united goal."

"Are we truly?" asked Senator Leeds. "It seems like at least one of us is working towards a more personal goal of becoming President and forgetting everything else."

"And you're not?" asked Shelby incredulously. "You're willing to work with those two morons to get in the line of secession? And what's this I hear about you resurrecting the so-called Anti-Strauss bill?"

"Is that true?" asked Strauss.

"I might need support for it as leverage to get back into the Secretary of State consideration," said Senator Leeds. "It won't pass, I can guarantee you that, but those two idiots both like the bill and if I show support for it, I could become a viable option for them as Secretary of State again."

"Assuming no one else on your staff commits murders in the next few days or weeks which seems highly unlikely," snorted Shelby.

"There are a few people who I wouldn't mind seeing die," said Senator Leeds staring coldly at Shelby. "And need I remind you that I was the only person available with people capable of carrying out those operations. It's not like you volunteered any of your people."

"My people would have handled things professionally," muttered Shelby. "I'd gladly send them on this type of a mission, but you jumped in before I had the chance."

"I'm sure your people could do better," said Leeds sarcastically.

Strauss sighed loudly and collapsed into his chair.

"This," said Strauss. "This is why I'm not good in groups. This petty infighting always breaks out and the goal gets lost. The three of us are in a unique position to move far closer to our goal than we've ever been before. All we need to do is to stay focused on the tasks at hand and we'll achieve our goal. Both of you want the presidency, but if need be I can see to it that neither of you get it. You're not the only options out there. Unless you pass that damned bill, and I'll destroy you if you try, I'll still have the power to handpick the next candidate. My groups hold over five billion dollars in support money for whoever I side with. They have over two hundred million members between them. I control those groups and to a large extent I control who wins every election in this country through those groups."

"Except this past one," muttered Shelby. "You backed the loser in that one."

"Harrison was a Republican and despite my support, many of the Democratic voters refused to vote for him. Given a viable Democratic candidate, one who doesn't get herself arrested and imprisoned before the election, I'd have given the big win to the Democratic ticket. As it was we almost kept Schwartz out. Those damned independents and cross-over voters killed us.

"If we're going to move this country in the right direction and become a single global community, then we've got to stop this petty infighting and bickering. If you two can't control yourselves then I'll find someone else who will do as they're told."

"I for one," said Senator Leeds, "am tired of being told what to do. I'm not a fucking puppet. You've been just giving us orders and expecting us to obey and frankly, I need more input into the decision-making process. Hell, we might be even farther along if you'd listened to me."

"I agree," said Shelby. "We need to be able to have input on what's said and done."

Strauss glared at the pair who refused to back down from his glare.

"I know what I'm doing!" said Strauss angrily. "I know what needs to be done! Both of you are blinded by your thirst for power. You've spent more time trying to destroy one another than our real enemies. I do listen to both of you, but both of you are trying more to achieve the presidency than the overall goal. We need to focus on the overall goal.

"Right now, both of you are severely damaged goods. Leeds, your people showing up dead at the scenes of murders is not helping you any. Shelby, those videos are killing you. I'm not sure the country would rally behind either of you for now."

"I've come back from worse," muttered Shelby.

"That's not exactly reassuring," muttered Leeds. "My story is already slipping from the headlines and will soon be forgotten."

"Thanks to the poison you leaked about me," muttered Shelby.

"Enough if this!" shouted Strauss. "Both of you grow up! Right now, at this moment, Shelby, you're not viable. Senator Leeds, I'm not sure how viable you are either, but you're better than Shelby at this moment. Work on those two morons and try to get the Secretary of State job. Shelby, keep your nose clean. I've got people trying to flush those videos off the online sites, but they're repopulating as quickly as we can get them down. If we can get the public to focus on something else for a bit, you could become viable once again. In either case, I need both of you.

"If we can get our hands on that Sara woman and get her to talk then there will be a special election and whichever one of you is the most viable at the time will get the nod. In the meantime, stop trying to destroy one another. And Senator, you can use that bill to try and get in with Schwartz, but if it passes, I'll destroy you in ways you can't even begin to imagine. I won't give up my power. Understand that. You cannot defeat me with legislation. Now both of you, get out of here. I've taken about all that I can of either of you."

* * *

Amy and Sara watched from the adjacent woods as the cars of Senator Leeds and Shelby left the Strauss compound.

"They didn't look very happy," muttered Amy.

"They all know they're being screwed," said Sara. "It's not a good spot to be in. Those videos are killing Shelby and the news reports about Leeds' associates have him worried. The divide and conquer strategy seems to be working well."

"In the divided sense, but what about the conquer?"

"We know how to get to Shelby. Leeds is no trouble to get to. What we need is a plan to get to Strauss. That's not going to be easy."

Indeed, Sara had brought them here to scout out the Strauss mansion and estate and what they'd seen was not encouraging. His estate encompassed over two hundred acres. Security gates and security fencing at two different levels protected those inside the mansion. A large, heavily armed security team prowled the grounds and there were even internal security guards should someone manage to reach the mansion. Unlike Shelby's security team, these guards were fed by the in-house staff which also numbered more than ten and would present an additional challenge to get past.

"What do you know about Strauss?" asked Sara.

"I don't know a lot about him, but I might know a guy who knows everything about him. Hidden deep within the FBI is a small group of agents devoted to rooting out corruption in politics. Among the things they look for are the big financial players and from what I've gathered, that team has, or had, someone on the inside of Strauss's staff. I know the guy who's been rumored to be their plant. His name is Henry Martin. He and Paul were good friends at the academy and stayed in touch. I might just be able to reach out to him for information."

"Does he know you didn't kill Paul?"

"I like to think so, but with the attention that got, I'm not so sure. I'll have to be careful about contacting him. It's probably best if I do this alone."

"Just don't do anything stupid. We need info on Strauss, but not if it gets you arrested or killed."

"I'll be careful. If there's a weakness in Strauss's defenses though, this guy will know it. We have the intercepts to show that Strauss was in on the plan to murder Paul and frame me for it, so I can use that to help convince him. The last I knew he hated Strauss with a passion, but still worked undercover and hid his hatred. If we could get rid of Strauss for him, it might make him very happy."

Amy watched from the other side of the street as Henry Martin entered the gym for his morning workout. She used the spoofer they'd picked up in NY to unlock his car door and she left a message for him on the front seat, placed a thicker message under the passenger seat then closed and locked the door and retreated to a nearby parking lot where she could observe his reaction.

It was about forty-five minutes later when he came out and found the note.

"What the hell?" he muttered after reading it. He pulled out his cellular phone and dialed the number on the note.

"Hi, Henry," said Amy.

"What the fuck are you doing?"

"I need your help."

"Fuck that! You killed Paul, now you want my help?"

"I didn't kill Paul. I was being set up to make it look like a murder-suicide. The two guys found dead in the apartment weren't good Samaritans who just happened upon the killing. They were the ones who'd shot Paul and were holding my gun in my mouth and forcing my hand onto the trigger. Someone came along and took them out, saving my life. George Strauss was one of those setting me up. I need to clear my name and I need your help to do so."

"Turn yourself in and let the bureau sort everything out."

"You know they'll just look for the easy answer and nail me. The guys behind this have big-time political cover. Strauss is one of them. That's why I need your help."

"Are you freaking kidding me?"

"Think of it as an early Christmas present. I know you're close to Strauss. I need your help."

"What do you need?" asked Henry.

"There's a manila envelope under the passenger seat with all of the details."

Amy watched as Henry extracted the envelope and read the contents.

"Seriously?" asked Henry after reading through it twice.

"I couldn't be more serious," said Amy.

"Okay. I'll see what I can do. There are no guarantees though."

* * *

Amy returned to the safe house to fill in Sara.

"Henry says George Strauss gives nearly his whole staff, including the security detail, Christmas day off. Only one older cook who's been with him forever stays on and he only stays as he has no other family. Strauss is a big old softie when it comes to Christmas. He leaves himself vulnerable. That's when we need to make our move."

"We'll have to see if he still does that this year," reminded Sara. "He may be changing his plans."

"It's an easy thing to observe. We stake out the place and see what happens. If they all leave, we make our move. If they stay in place, then we wait for another opportunity."

"Do you trust this Henry guy you met with?"

"I trust him enough to believe him on this. He wants Strauss dead as much as we do."

Sara pondered the situation and agreed to stake out the Strauss mansion starting Christmas eve and see what happened. If the guards and staff all left, as this Henry claimed, then it might be their best opportunity to make a move.

* * *

Sara watched with amazement as one by one the cars filed out of the Strauss estate until only one single car remained. The last guards to leave padlocked the gates and then drove off. There were no more foot patrols and no one other than Strauss and his old cook left in the house.

"That's pretty impressive," muttered Sara.

"Henry didn't let me down," said Amy. "What say we go pay Mr. Strauss a visit?"

"Let's just keep an eye on things for a few minutes first," said Sara. "I'm not sure I believe our good fortune."

For another full half-hour, Sara watched as Strauss moved about the house, but no one else was in sight. He finally settled in his first-floor office and seemed to be napping in a recliner there.

"Okay," said Sara. "Let's see what happens."

She hopped over the fence and then helped Amy across. They traversed the area between the two lines of fencing and then climbed the second row of fencing. The house was just a few hundred yards away now and George Strauss was still napping in his chair. A large gift-wrapped present sat atop the desk.

Sara dashed across the open yard to the door leading to the office and checked it. It was unlocked. She opened the door and slid n followed by Amy and was thinking to herself that, "This was too easy."

That's when she felt Amy's gun press into the small of her back.

"Keep your hands where I can see them," ordered Amy. "I don't want to have to shoot you, but I will if need be. A shot here won't kill you, but it'll cripple you. You don't want that."

George Strauss was now sitting upright in his recliner with a big smile on his face and applauding Amy as another man came from the side and placed handcuffs on Sara.

"You betrayed me?" asked Sara of Amy.

"She sold you to me for ten million dollars and a promise to clear her name," said George Strauss. "A small price I must say and arguably the best Christmas present I've ever gotten. The infamous Sara X cuffed and about to tell me all that she knows. I couldn't ask for a better present."

"And my money?" asked Amy.

"In the gift-wrapped package on my desk. You can count it if you'd like but it will take some time to count ten million dollars."

"And my name and reputation?"

"They will be cleared within a day or two. Fresh eyes will investigate the shooting of your Paul and find that he was shot by the two thugs who were found dead. They'll find that you confronted them and took them down. You fled because you were aware there were more of them nearby but have been secretly working with the FBI since then to pin things down. You'll be a hero, my girl. You'll get your old job back and likely a promotion.

"I must say, I was wondering how we were ever going to trap the infamous Sara X, then Amy reaches out to Henry here with this plan and it worked out perfectly.

"Silly girl. You thought you'd take me down? You have no idea what you're up against."

"What exactly am I up against then?" asked Sara.

George Strauss laughed and then smiled before replying.

"You're fighting a fight you cannot possibly win. I'm but one of hundreds, if not thousands, or tens of thousands who stand in your way. We're not like you. You're a peasant. We're the elite. We are the ruling class. It is our destiny to rule over the likes of you. We are building a global empire that we will rule over and nothing will get in our way."

"It's kind of hard to build things when you're dead."

"You could kill ten thousand of us and another ten thousand would rise to take our place. Empire building is a cause that cannot be destroyed. If you had succeeded in striking me down tonight, it would have changed nothing. My predecessors go back through history to the time of the Romans who built the then greatest empire ever. We were part of the building of the British empire. In World War Two we were behind the Axis empire. We had our hands in the making of the Soviet empire. And now, we are working on a new global empire."

"You may not have noticed this, but all of those empires have fallen."

"But, we have learned from those failures. We have tools now that were unimaginable back then. We can maintain surveillance on those who wish to disrupt our plans. We can stop any insurrection before it gets a foothold. We will not fail."

"Why not just be happy with how things are?"

"Because we deserve to rule. We're better than the likes of you. Admit it, you felt compelled to bow before me. You felt my power. You knew you were in the presence of greatness. You, and those like you, will bow before us and pay us the respect we deserve. Well, you would if you were to survive tonight.

"Henry, if you'd be so kind as to take our guest downstairs to the private lockup we have down there. And, be careful, she's a tricky one this one. I'll be informing Shelby of her capture. I'd promised to let Shelby be here to assist int eh questioning of our dear Sara."

"Yes, sir," said Henry giving a short bow as he grabbed Sara by the handcuffs and pulled her away.

Henry led Sara out of the room and to a nearby staircase that led downstairs. They were nearly to the basement when they heard the gunshots.

* * *

Amy had opened the present to be sure the cash was there and then nodded to George Strauss.

"You're sure my reputation will be cleared after this?"

"My girl, you could run for president after this and no one could find any dirt on you. Your name will be sparkling. I must say, I'm quite impressed with how you pulled this all off. Getting her to agree to come here and then turning her over to me was a stroke of genius. I was a tad nervous about sending my security team away, but Henry assured me I could trust you, so I did. And it's paid off brilliantly."

"Sara's not stupid. She'd never come here if your full security team was in place. You're pretty much impossible to reach with them in place. We needed to get you to let your guard down though to get close to you. And we succeeded."

"Indeed, you did, my girl. Indeed, you did."

"And now I can kill you myself for what you ordered done to Paul."

Strauss looked up to find Amy's gun pointed at his head.

"What is this?" demanded Strauss.

"It's a trap, but not for Sara. And guess what? You got caught."

"You don't have to do this," begged Strauss. "I can give you anything you want!"

"I just want you dead."

Amy fired two shots into his head then stood over his fallen body and fired two more shots ensuring that George Strauss was gone.

* * *

"That took long enough," muttered Henry after hearing the shots. He undid Sara's handcuffs and handed her back her gun.

"What's happening?" asked Sara as Henry pulled a gun of his own and started to lead them back upstairs.

"Amy's plan worked to get her alone with Strauss so she could kill him, but the guards aren't far away. There's a pair of them hidden upstairs and the rest are waiting down the road to get a call to come back. The guards upstairs almost certainly heard the gunshots and are heading our way. We've got to move fast if any of us are to get out of here alive."

The footsteps of the guards from upstairs could be heard racing down the stairs, so Sara and Henry took positions and shot the pair as they turned the corner. Amy came towards them after that and explained.

"Sorry about that, but I'll explain it all later if we live long enough."

"I've kind of got it figured out," said Sara. "You and Henry conspired to make it look like you were turning me in, then gunned down Strauss. I'd kind of liked to have been in on the plan though."

Henry now stepped past Amy and led them to a cabinet under the stairs where he unlocked an electronic lock and swung the door open.

"Pick your poison," said Henry stepping back and letting the two women see the weapons hidden inside the closet.

"Now we're talking," said Sara taking up a fully automatic M-16 from the closet.

"Grab some spare clips," said Henry. "We're likely to need them. There are nineteen guards in total. There were the two upstairs and seventeen more who were camped out down the road. We're going to have to fight our way out of here and it's not going to be easy. The good news is we're in the right place. The house and grounds have been built to withstand a pitched battle. We've got better fields of fire than they do, and they must expose themselves to head this way."

"And local law enforcement?" asked Sara.

"Can't get past the outermost gates," said Henry. "God willing, we'll melt into the woods once we deal with this initial counter-attack and be gone before the locals can get involved."

Henry nodded to the nearby windows.

"Get in position. The guards will be arriving soon. I'll hit the grounds' lights and they'll be easy pickings. There should be another seventeen coming. Once we're sure they're down, we get the hell out of here."

"Good plan," said Sara taking a position near one of the windows he indicated while Amy did likewise. Both raised the windows enough to get their gun barrels out and then waited for something to move.

"They're coming," said Sara as she saw a hint of movement in the near-total darkness.

"Close your eyes for a second then," said Henry as he opened a panel near the door and hit some switches.

The blackness disappeared in a blink and the grounds were lit up like a ballpark. The guards who had been using the darkness for cover now found themselves exposed and vulnerable. Amy opened fire first and with her first burst, five guards fell. Sara followed suit and took down a further seven. The two combined to take down the last five, two of whom were retreating to the woods as they were gunned down.

"Time to go then," said Henry turning off the powerful overhead lights once more and opening the door. Sara hurried out and took a defensive position and then looked back for Amy and Henry. She was about to go back to get them when she saw Amy had grabbed the ten million dollars in cash from the desk and was bringing it with her.

"Seriously?" asked Sara.

"It's for Henry," said Amy. "His reward for the job."

"Where is Henry?" asked Sara.

"Just had to grab this," said Henry handing Sara a bag containing several portable hard drives."

"What's in this?" asked Sara as she took the bag.

"Dear old George didn't trust anyone, so he videotaped every meeting with everyone without their knowledge. On those hard drives are enough videos of meetings with Strauss to put half of DC in prison for the next fifty years."

Amy handed the ten million to Henry and said," You deserve this."

"Hell, I'd have killed the old goat for free given the chance, but I appreciate the cash. Let's just focus on getting out of here now though."

Sara led them across the now dark grounds. A few of the guards could be heard groaning in pain, but they ignored them as they made their way to the first fence. All three made it over and then to the second fence and over that as well. Sara led the way to their car and the three climbed in.

"Keep the guns handy," said Sara. "I'm guessing there might be a roadblock or two on our way out of here."

The guns weren't necessary however as the police hadn't yet responded to the sounds of the gunshots. Living in a very remote location meant no neighbors were near enough to know for sure where the shots had come from. By the time the police had figured it out, Sara, Henry, and Amy were well out of danger.

Henry directed them to where his getaway car had been stashed and then climbed out with the package of cash.

"Ladies, it's been fun. But, let's not do this again."

"I owe you big time," said Amy.

"No, I did that for Paul and the others like him who those bastards have taken out. I dare say our old friend Mr. Strauss is having a pretty interesting discussion right now with whoever's in control of the golden gates these days."

"Lay low for a while," said Sara.

"I will," said Henry as he walked away and the other two headed back towards Sara's safe house.

"If you ever lie to me like that again, I will kill you," said Sara.

"I had to," said Amy. "I didn't think you'd ever agree to this plan since you didn't know Henry. I knew and trusted Henry to go along with it, but I knew there was no way I could get you to go along with it. It worked out okay."

"You killed Strauss, but we had to kill or injure a lot of other people too. I'd far prefer to just take him out."

"It was impossible though. He's never unguarded. This was the only way. Remember, I talked about making a deal with him? You were the only thing I could offer him that might entice him into making a move like this. He was sure Henry was loyal and with the two guards upstairs and the rest a short distance away, he felt safe making the deal. He trusted me to want to clear my name and make ten million in the process. To him, money and reputation were more important than anything else. It made my offer an easy sell. He assumed I wanted my name cleared and the ten million. He bought the story and we nailed him."

* * *

The news of the murder of George Strauss and the wounding or killing if his entire security team, made major shockwaves. Nowhere were those shockwaves felt more strongly than in the homes of Senator Leeds and Shelby Johnson.

"How the fuck did she do that?" demanded Leeds.

"She's good," said Shelby.

"No one's that good. There were what, nineteen or twenty guards at the place? Against one woman? What the hell happened?"

"Strauss called me early in the day Christmas and told me he was getting us all a great present. He wouldn't go into details on the phone, but I got the vibe he thought he was getting Sara."

"Yeah, well she got him instead."

"The initial ballistics report says it was the gun of that missing FBI agent Amy Jeter that fired the shots that killed Strauss. The guards were gunned down with M-16's from the looks of things. Strauss had an armory in his house for his guards and it appears some of those weapons were used to take out the guards."

"How many people were with her?"

"I don't know, but the FBI agent was there. They say one of Strauss's aides is missing. He may have worked with the other two in carrying out the attack."

"Son of a bitch! I assume the authorities are looking for the guy?"

"Yeah, the same they're looking for Sara and that Amy Jeter. You've seen how effective that is."

"What the fuck do we do now? Strauss being dead kind of kills most of our plans. I'm sure as hell not getting the Secretary of State job and the odds of a special election being called now are gone."

"The special election might not be completely dead. If we can tie the Strauss killing to Sara and then tie her to those two idiots, we might still pull off the special election."

"You're dreaming. We've been listening to everything those two have been saying and they've said nothing about Strauss. How the hell do we tie any of that to them?"

"I don't know. We have to hope they make a mistake."

Leeds paced the floor nervously and then nodded outside Shelby's house to the guards.

"Do you trust them to keep you safe?"

"They'll keep me safe or die trying," said Shelby. "Between the guards out front and the dogs in the back, I'm safe enough. If Sara or her new friend try to get in here, those guys should buy me enough time to slip into the safe room if nothing else. I can outlast anyone in there."

"I may just start living in my safe room."

"There's something seriously wrong with this world when people like us have to hide out from the likes of them."

"Something that we can fix when we get power. A global government with a single police force using the full surveillance powers that are now available will help to quash any insurgents like Sara and put them away before they can do much harm. Once we build our new empire, we'll be unstoppable.

"Things like this Sara and our idiotic new president Schwartz are just hiccups along the road. We'll achieve our goals. We'll create our worldwide empire. There are too many of us who know how amazing that can be for us to fail."

* * *

Amy and Sara had been staked out in the parking lot since ten in the morning waiting for the day's first deliveries to go out.

"Here he comes," said Sara nodding to the delivery driver walking out of the takeout with several bags of food. "Are you ready?"

"More than ready," said Amy watching the readout on the spoofer, "I've got it."

"Are you sure?"

"Let's check and find out," said Amy. She waited until the delivery truck was backing up and she hit the button to unlatch the back hatch. The hatch flew open and the driver stopped the truck, got out, and closed the hatch again before driving off.

"Part one is a go, how's your tracker working?"

Sara had planted a GPS tracker on the truck the night before and she opened her laptop and checked the signal. The truck was clearly shown as it made its way on the first of the deliveries.

"We're good," said Sara.

"Then let's get his show on the road."

* * *

Luis Ribeiro loaded up his supper deliveries for the Johnson estate and smiled to himself. The Russian guards weren't much for conversation, but they were big tippers and he liked that.

The drive to the Johnson estate took about fifteen minutes but it was an easy drive along quiet roads. He might only see a couple of other cars once he got out of town. He was just a couple of miles away from the estate when he saw her up ahead. A young blond wearing a tennis outfit with a short skirt was standing alongside a car that was half on and half off the road with a flat left rear tire. As he neared he watched as she kicked the now flat tire then hopped on one leg in obvious pain from the kick. She saw him coming and flagged him down. Luis pulled over behind her and stopped. She started to hop towards him on her good foot, then stopped and leaned against the trunk of her car and motioned for him to come to her as she flexed the foot she'd kicked the tire with.

Luis climbed down from the truck and made his way to the woman.

"Having trouble?"

"Like you wouldn't believe," muttered Amy. "Do you know how to change a tire by any chance?"

"I sure do," said Luis. "But, I've got to make a delivery first."

"Will it take long?" asked Amy as she ran her hands up and down her injured leg.

"No, maybe five minutes then I can be back," said Luis watching appreciatively as Amy's hands stroked her leg.

"I'll owe you so much," said Amy with a suggestive smile. "I'm not sure how I can repay you."

Luis had a few ideas in mind as he watched her continue to stroke her leg, but he'd explore those options later.

"Let me make my delivery then I'll be back to help you out. It won't take long."

"Thank you so much," said Amy. "I appreciate this."

"It's no problem."

Luis got back into his truck and drove off hurriedly to finish his delivery and get back to earn his reward. Amy waved goodbye as he drove off then he was around the corner and out of sight.

Amy was opening the trunk and removing the air pump when Sara rejoined her and put the spoofer into the trunk.

"We'd better hurry," said Sara. "Loverboy won't dawdle with you waiting here."

"Only we won't be here," said Amy as she attached the air pump to the deflated tire and started inflating it. "This only takes about a minute to refill and then we'll be gone. Did you get the sedatives planted?"

"Yeah, it was easy. Within a half-hour, we'll be able to do anything we want to do."

The tire was soon inflated, and the air pump put away. Sara got behind the wheel and drove them down a dirt path that paralleled the Johnson estate. Shortly after entering the path, they saw the delivery truck speed back to the stranded motorist.

"He's going to be pissed when you're not there," said Sara.

"Not my problem," said Amy who was shedding the tennis outfit for more practical clothes for the next stage of the operation. They parked the car along the path and then made their way through the woods to the fence surrounding the Johnson estate.

"I'll handle the dogs out back and meet you inside," said Amy.

"I'll make sure the guards are down, either drugged or dealt with, then find Shelby before she can retreat to her safe room and detain her until you show up."

Sara then left and staying in the woods walked along the fence line until she could see the guard station. The guards were not visible. She quickly scaled the fence and hurried to the station with her pistol in hand, but it was unnecessary. Both guards were knocked out. She then sprinted towards the door and structure that had been placed there to house the remaining guards and found them also unconscious. She then checked the door and slid into the house itself.

Shelby's voice could be heard in a nearby room and Sara could see her with her back turned, talking to someone on the phone. Sara slid back and waited for the conversation to end then entered the room with her pistol pointed directly at Shelby.

"Surprise!" said Sara as Shelby turned and stared at her in horror.

"How did you get in here?" demanded Shelby. "What have you done with my guards?"

"They got a bit sleepy after their dinnertime and are taking a nice long nap."

"You drugged them?"

"Just a little. They'll be fine in ten hours or so. I can't say the same for you though."

"So, you're going to shoot me then? This is how this all ends?"

"I'll only shoot you if I have to. I understand you've installed a safe room. Care to show it to me?"

"You want a house tour now?" asked Shelby incredulously.

"It looks like a nice place. It may be coming on the market soon. I could use a place like this to settle down. Who better to show me around than you? Now, about this safe room?"

"It's adjacent to my bedroom."

"Lead the way."

Shelby was more than a little surprised by this turn of events, but if she could reach the saferoom and get inside it before Sara could harm her, she might just live through this. Once inside, the safe room was largely impenetrable. She just needed a way to get inside and then get the door closed before Sara could kill her.

Shelby led the way upstairs to her opulent bedroom and then across the room to what appeared to be a blank wall. Hidden in the chair rail molding of the room was a switch that would activate the door and unlock it. She swung the door open and stepped inside. A quick attempt to shut the door was rebuffed by Sara who shoved Shelby into the room. It was a smallish space, maybe six feet wide by ten feet deep with a small bed along one wall.

"Sit on the bed," ordered Sara as she surveyed the room.

Shelby obeyed as she looked for an opportunity to make a move and close the door. Then she heard it. Someone else was coming. A smile flitted across Shelby's face as she assumed one of her guards had survived. That smile soon disappeared when she saw Amy with the four of the guard dogs on leashes joining Sara at the door.

"Took you long enough," said Sara.

"Sorry, but I think two of these guys are gay. They keep trying to mount one another and getting them up here without an incident was a tad more challenging than I'd assumed."

Shelby was horrified to see the dogs. She'd seen them take down a deer that had wandered onto the grounds and tear it apart. They were vicious and even her guards feared them.

"What are they doing here?" asked Shelby with fear in her voice.

"They're here to dispense justice," said Sara. She looked as Amy had the dogs all in sit and stay position and was undoing their leashes. "You don't know much Russian by any chance, do you?"

"No," said Shelby watching in amazement as these wild and seemingly uncontrollable dogs were licking Amy's face and wagging their tails as she whispered to them.

"Pity for you then," said Sara as she stepped back and nodded to Amy.

Amy pointed to the bed and Shelby and gave the attack command in Russian to the dogs. As the dogs lunged towards Shelby, Sara calmly closed and locked the safe room door. Shelby's screams were soon drowned out by the thick walls and Sara and Amy exchanged a high five.

"Do you think that's too cruel?" asked Sara.

"Seriously? After all she's done?"

"I was talking about for the dogs."

Amy laughed before replying.

"No, they've got a hundred and eighty pounds of fresh meat to eat. They'll be fine."

"I guess so," said Sara. "Let's get out of here. We've got one-third of their triumvirate to still clear up."

* * *

It wasn't long before the death of Shelby Johnson at the hands of her guard dogs dominated the news headlines. What remains there were of her had to be sent out for DNA testing as the mass of meat and rotting flesh that had been finally found in the safe room was unidentifiable.

"So much for the safety of the fucking safe room," muttered Senator Leeds as he switched off the news and grimaced as he imagined Shelby's last minutes. His security was now all he focused on and nothing else mattered, but he knew it was largely a hopeless task. Sara had gotten to both Strauss and Shelby despite their precautions and it was unlikely anything he could do would be even equal to what they'd presented.

While Leeds had always known he'd die eventually, he hadn't ever really confronted the reality of it happening this soon. He pondered his options. He could run. Take his money and flee the country for someplace safe, but where was safe? Where could he be out of reach of this Sara creature? No. Escape wasn't an option.

Could he make a deal with her? Have her spare his life in exchange for something? But, what could he offer her? She had money and seemingly all the power she wanted. What could he offer her?

His security team leader then knocked on his office door and told him a package had arrived.

"What is it?" asked Leeds.

"A cellular phone. We've checked it out and it's not been poisoned or tampered with in any way. It's safe."

"Thank you," said Leeds dismissing the guard. He had little doubt who'd sent the phone to him. So little in fact that when it rang he answered with, "Hello, Sara."

"Senator," said Sara. "I trust you've been watching the news."

"I'm assuming I'm next in line. That was an absurdly cruel way to kill Shelby, by the way. Would you mind something less distasteful for me?"

"It doesn't have to end like that," said Sara. "If you resign and step aside, admit to your crimes, and accept your punishment, this could all end easily for you. You'd spend the rest of your life in prison, but you'd live."

"I'd rather die. I've committed far fewer crimes than you have and yet you get to live free while I spend my days in prison? How about we both come forward and confess all of our crimes together."

"That's not going to happen."

"So, what happens now? Do you choose which of you gets to kill me?"

"Death is too easy of a way out for you I'm afraid," said Sara. "We have other ways of destroying you."

"What other ways?"

"Did you know Strauss recorded all of your meetings? He viewed it as an insurance policy of sorts should something happen to him. Guess who has those recordings now?"

"No," said Leeds. "He wasn't that stupid."

"He was. He thought he lived in an impenetrable fortress with enough security, and the data would be kept safe. We penetrated his security and the data is now in our hands. Those videos could go public very shortly and you could be in a lot of trouble."

"Could?" asked Leeds.

"Just could," said Sara with a smile. "You see, I have two friends who were recently elected to high office who need support. If a certain high-ranking Senator were to support them unconditionally in their goals, those videos might just stay private. You'd have to twist a few arms to get things done they want done and use your influence and power over your fellow party members and allies, but you'd have value to me then."

"You're blackmailing me?"

"I'm giving you a choice. There are three options. You can keep your job and its perks and work with Benjamin and Charlie. I could kill you. Or, I could expose your little coup alliance and the Strauss videos. Those videos make a very solid case for treason and the penalty for treason is death. In two of those scenarios, you end up dead with your reputation destroyed. In one you live and get to be part of the team that's going to change how business is done from now on in Washington. The choice is yours. If you make the right choice, they could end up carving your face in Mount Rushmore down the road. Make the wrong choice and your name will be carved in a tombstone."

"Seriously? You'll let me live if I agree to work with those two?"

"I will, but you can't just be a token vote in their favor. You must devote your life to fulfilling their goals. If I ever feel that you're giving anything less than a hundred percent effort, then I will destroy you, one way or the other. I own you, Senator Leeds. As uncomfortable as that is for you, it's better than being dead. Benjamin and Charlie need allies to achieve their goals. You'd be a powerful ally to them."

"What guarantee do I have that this is real?"

"None. Just know that you're more valuable to me alive and working with my guys than dead. If you aren't working for them, then you have no value to me. I'll be sending you an edited video of some of the clips of you, Shelby, and Strauss meeting in his office. You'll want to watch those before you decide. And don't even think about just running off. I can find you wherever you go."

"You're giving me no real choice here. I'll work with your guys. I'll damned near kill myself to get their stuff through the Senate, but I can't make any guarantees that others will go along with me."

"You'd be surprised to find how many people I know who are pretty influential and owe me favors," said Sara. "You do your part and let me worry about the rest. Do we have a deal?"

Senator Leeds hesitated for just a moment before nodding his head and telling Sara yes that they had a deal. Sara then hung up the phone and threw away the burner phone she'd been using. She climbed back into her car and drove back to the safe house where Amy was waiting for her.

"I don't like letting him live," said Amy.

"Benjamin and Charlie need him. The good news is we own him now. If he makes even one mistake, we expose his secrets and destroy him. He's a powerful tool for our side."

"Still, it irks me that he's alive, Paul's dead, and I'm still on the run."

"You won't be on the run for long," said Sara. "You just need to lie low for a few more weeks."

"Why?"

"We're just a few more weeks from the inauguration. The out-going president still has a lot of power including the power to pardon. Word on the street is you'll be getting a full pardon from him and returned to your duties."

"The out-going president will pardon me? Why?"

"Because it would look bad for Benjamin to do it as soon as he takes office. The out-going president owes me a favor or two also, so I pulled a few strings. Once Benjamin takes office you'll get a rather large promotion."

"Seriously?"

"How's the title of Madam Director of the FBI strike you?"

"No fucking way!"

"It's good to have friends in high places."

"I'll never get confirmed."

"I've got more power around this town than you might think. You'll get confirmed. Certain narratives are being created to explain everything that went down. You'll come out of this a hero and the first female Director of the FBI. Oh, and if you run into any trouble anytime, don't forget that Strauss made videos of all his meetings with his Washington allies, not just his coup partners. If anyone gets too out of line questioning what happened, let me know and I'll remind them of what was said in those supposedly private meetings."

A flash of recognition crossed Amy's face.

"That's why the out-going president owes you?"

"Suffice to say he and Mr. Strauss said some things in their private meetings that would damage his legacy in a very, very big way."

"Shit! I owe you."

"Just keep your guys and gals at the FBI from tracking me down. I'm going back into retirement and would prefer not to be hunted down by the Feds."

"We couldn't find you even if we tried."

"Yeah, well, don't try. I need some time off."

"Madam Director?"

"Has a nice ring to it doesn't it? It should also help keep Leeds in line knowing that you're heading the agency that could put him away."

"The rest of those videos, any chance I can see them?"

"It's probably better if you don't. Suffice to say I'll be keeping them someplace nice and safe. Oh, and if you ever get any ideas about hunting me down, remember that your shooting of Strauss is on the videos also. Seeing the Director of the FBI accepting a ten-million-dollar payment then gunning down Strauss would not be good for your career."

"You'd play that card against me?"

"I do what I have to do to survive. It's how I stay alive. As for now, I need some time off and to get away from things. I think we've got Benjamin and Charlie set up nicely to succeed. You'll soon be out of trouble and in a good spot. Your friend Henry is off spending his ten million someplace, and two of the three bad guys are dead with the third one in our undying debt. All in all, I think we're about done here."

Amy shook her head in amazement and then nodded.

"It's been a hell of a couple of weeks," said Amy.

"Sadly, things don't stay quiet around me for long. Hopefully, that'll all be changing soon. Lay low for a bit until the pardon. You'll be contacted soon with the narrative of what happened. Memorize it and follow it and you'll be fine. Hell, you'll be a national hero."

"For killing someone," mused Amy. "Granted he deserved it, but still."

"It's a strange world sometimes. Just take care of yourself. And don't try to track me down. You won't find me, but I'll find out you're trying, and I don't want to have to come after you. I need some downtime."

"Agreed. And I sure don't want you coming after me. I've seen how you work. You're too good to cross."

"You're not bad yourself. And one final time, I'm sorry I couldn't get there in time to save Paul."

"Shit happens. That'll leave a hole in my heart for a while, but if history is any indicator that should heal."

"You might want to look up Henry when that hole heals. I kind of got the vibe from him that he's into you. You'd make a heck of a pair."

"Henry? I'd never really thought of him that way."

"I've seen how he looks at you. He's thought of you that way. It's just something to keep in mind. He's someone you could share your past with and be comfortable knowing what you know of his past. Just don't team up against me."

"Never!"

"I'll be seeing you around Madam Director. You're going to make one hell of an FBI Director. Benjamin and Charlie will need you as they buck the system. Washington doesn't like change and those two are looking to make big changes. They'll make lots of enemies along the way. Keep them safe. I like those two old codgers."

Sara then left the safe house for the final time knowing she could never return to it and hoping she'd never need to.

Author's notes

Thanks for reading this book. I hope you enjoyed it.

You can find out more information about me and my books at my Amazon Author page at: https://www.amazon.com/-/e/B007SB0GJY or my Goodreads author page at: https://www.goodreads.com/author/show/8247851.Donald_Shinn

Made in United States
North Haven, CT
09 December 2025